the 826 Quarterly

AN 826 VALENCIA ORIGINAL
Published October 2011
as the 14th edition of the *826 Quarterly*.
Created by all hands on deck at 826 Valencia.

826 Valencia Street
San Francisco, California 94110
826valencia.org

EDITOR Justin Carder
MANAGING EDITORS Amy Langer & McKenna Stayner
ART DIRECTION María Inés Montes
BOOK AND COVER DESIGN Otis Pig
ILLUSTRATIONS Lisa Brown
COPY EDITOR Oriana Leckert
THE *826 QUARTERLY* EDITORIAL BOARD Amy Langer, McKenna Stayner, Gina
Cargas, Arty Zhang, Paolo Yumol, Tino Mori

PLEASE VISIT:
The Pirate Store at 826
826valencia.org/store

ISBN 978-1-934750-26-1
Printed in Canada by The Prolific Group.
Distributed by Publishers Group West

the 826 Quarterly

VOLUME 14 * Fall 2011

*Published twice yearly, at least.

Contents

About 826 Valencia

Foreword

LISA BROWN ✳ *Author & Illustrator*

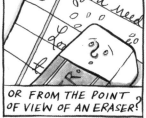

Editorial Board Intros

PAOLO YUMOL ✳ *age 16*
Lick-Wilmerding High School

TINO MORI ✳ *age 16*
Palo Alto High School

ARTY ZHANG ✳ *age 17*
Lowell High School

SWEAT

At the age of sixteen, I have a certain sweat, the sweat you get when people look you up and down on the sidewalk and start mumbling things to themselves, sure you're on your way to do something illegal or somehow distasteful. It's the sweat you get when you realize that you spend too much of your time taking showers and talking to yourself. Most importantly, it's the sweat you get when you start to wonder if you will ever be taken seriously by anyone else in your entire life.

Working for the *826 Quarterly* Ed Board is a way of suppressing that sweat, even if naïvely, for just an hour or two. I'd like to think that we are simultaneously helping steer younger children as far away from that sweat and fear as possible; they see their names published in a real, honest-to-life book, and suddenly life has meaning. They have a reason to wake up in the morning when us sixteen- and seventeen-year-olds might be otherwise feebly grasping at straws, a reason that's tangible and unquestionable and sophisticated in a childlike sort of way. Their eyes might dilate, or they might drool a little bit at the corners of their mouths.

In any case, is there any other way to live life besides sitting on a couch alongside Tino and Arty and Gina and Amy and McKenna, wheezing, reading newspaper articles named "What's the Deal with Dogs?" in which eight-year-olds bark at us through the page? Stories about marbles with souls, poetry about whale houses in the year 2030? Literature that makes you sweat in a good way, in a way you never really understood but always dreamed about.

- Paolo Yumol

* * *

LIKE A BEACON OF AWESOME

Chances are, you're reading this by accident. Let's be honest; introductions are like legal documents for your cellular telephone. You feel you should read them, but really, who has the time?

Perhaps you're flicking through the pages of this anthology in search of the first piece—standing awkwardly in a bookstore, trying to decide whether or not to buy this book (the answer to your quandary is yes, by the way). You could be anywhere. It doesn't really matter. My point is, if you've read this far, there must be something wrong with you.

Now, unlike this introduction—which was thrown together with as much care as my famous "whatever's in the fridge" casserole, this Quarterly is something else. Something magnificent, in fact, like a beacon of awesome. The fine editing/review board selected these wonderful pieces from our trove of youth literature, not unlike a monkey picking its mate for lice. Only we didn't proceed to eat the selected submissions.

Our splendid crew really did everything from reading the pieces to re-reading them. Each session was a collage of gut instinct, peppered with the occasional piece of logic and wisdom. Did I mention we had cookies? We really had quite the A-Team assembled.

A QUICK SIDENOTE: I find the label "A-Team" offensive, as it discriminates against the other letters in the alphabet. Don't be complacent in the face of discrimination.

We had several great adventures as the editing/review board, such as ordering coffee and taking fifteen-minute breaks between long discussions.

As for the actual stories, I think you will enjoy our panoply of delicious youth literature—like jam cookies filled with happiness. I know some of these wonderful writers personally, who created such works of art. Some pieces will make you think. Some will make you laugh. Some may make you think about laughing, while others still will make you laugh about thinking. Such is the power of the writer. So, without further ado, and with all the enthusiasm of a WalMart employee—I welcome you to the *826 Quarterly, Volume 14*! Enjoy.

- Tino Mori

* * *

TWO BATHROOMS, BOTH ALIKE IN DIGNITY

There are two (somewhat public) bathrooms at 826 Valencia. The first, by far the most widely accepted, somehow, through the dual tricks of lighting and a giant gilded mirror, gives off the impression of being golden. A partial list of various framed pictures on the walls include a unicorn playing the piano, his mane stylishly waving to the inexorable ebb and flow of his music; a ghost with ice cream bemoaning his lack of companionship to a kind of lizard; and a dinosaur chewing bubblegum carrying a ninja.

The second bathroom is a sickly brown. It possesses a single window overlooking some trash bins. (It also has a towel dispenser, but the first bathroom has one as well.)

Editing is kind of like that.

Bear with me for a moment. Step into the gilded bathroom as a student for a second, as a million have done before us, and think of their imaginations seeping out, racing and bouncing off the walls before being sucked up by the ventilation. You have stepped into a world rife with werewolves and exploding kitchens, where the world is hopeless and the mounts in the distance are covered by pollution and warfare because she dumped you, and the only dignified response left is to write stories about deposed kings and card games on which the fate of the world rests. Where we can ride off in spaceships and live in trees afterward.

Now, as an adult, pick up the bag of used paper towels and head to the other bathroom next to the trash bins. Step inside; there's a message above the toilet (probably recycled from the first bathroom) warning against careless disposal of brown paper, exploding toilets, and no time to linger.

Unfold those papers you brought along, the runoff of the imaginations that were transcribed into text and merely a weak facsimile of those myriad fancies and convictions, and here's what editing feels like: to sit in one restroom and read messages from the other side, waiting for your epiphany and insight as to what to do, and feeling at once that you can find God in the toilet and a fear that you might delete Shakespeare in the making.

- Arty Zhang

Every day, zillions of items go missing—that pink sock your mom bought you for Valentine's Day, the 1954 penny from your pocket, the bobby pin that kept that one stray hair out of your eyes. We lose these things, mourn them for a moment, and forget them. How could we be so cruel? Don't we know that objects have feelings too? In the Lost Objects workshop, taught by playwright and actress Sarah Savage, writers aged ten to twelve took on the role of these forgotten things to give readers a glimpse into what happens after that penny rolls down the drain.✱

Lost and Maybe Found

Stories of Lost Objects

You, the Marble

DIEGO PONCE ✶ *age 10*
St. Anthony's School

You. This story is about you. Don't worry, I won't say anything embarrassing. You can trust me, I swear. Okay, you trust me, right? If you don't, skip to the next story. I don't mind. You just don't know what you're missing.

You're a marble. A nice, pretty, shiny one. You have a beautiful coat of light, silky blue. You're your owner's prize marble. You're glorious, you're beautiful, and all that other good stuff. One day, you are taken out of your glass case. You take a look at the world around you. Until now, you had been locked in your glass case. It was stuffy in there. Now you can breathe, but not too well. Janeway, your owner, a sixth-grader, has no way of knowing that marbles can actually breathe. Oh, the agony!

On the bright side, you think, I am probably going to show-and-tell at Janeway's school. You're wrong. You're deadly wrong. Soon you are put down in the sand. Nice and soft, you say.

Then you are put in Janeway's hand. Her hand is in a strange arrangement. Suddenly, you are shot out of Janeway's hand, her thumb bashing into you.

You roll at top speed toward another marble. It looks as if he is saying his prayers.

You bash into each other. He is sent rolling out of a ring you noticed while still in Janeway's hand. You, however, stay in the place that the previous marble occupied. You look around. Ten of the eleven kids, including Janeway, are giving you a grand ovation. The eleventh kid is too stunned to speak, revenge in his gray, stony eyes. You don't care. You just stand and receive the claps, cheers, and hoots. Then the ovation stops.

The stony-eyed kid puts something round and tanned in his hand. You turn away. You're mad at him for ruining your ovation. You are suddenly knocked off balance out of the ring. When you finally stop rolling, you turn to see who knocked into you. You gasp. The tanned thing turns out to be—oh no—a marble!

You are suddenly picked up by a hand that is hard and stiff that feels nothing like Janeway's. You see the stony-eyed kid's face. You then turn to see Janeway bursting into tears. You meant so much to her.

You try to cry, but can't. You're too depressed. You wonder if there is a anti-depressant for marbles. You doubt it.

Suddenly the stony-eyed kid runs into his house. You get farther away from Janeway.

You are depressed until your depression is replaced with anger. You memorize the streets from the school to the stony-eyed kid's house. You know the way from Janeway's house to school. You overheard the directions back in the glass case, when Janeway invited her friend Lizzie over. The kid gets to his house. It is covered with bright purple paint. He rushes to his room and puts you on the windowsill.

"Joe!" someone hollers. It sounds like a female. "Get down here this instant, young man!" you hear.

Joe, the stony-eyed kid, rolls his eyes and heads downstairs. You notice that he left the window open. You make the dangerous decision to roll out onto the street.

As you're falling, you're thinking about the directions from Joe's house to Janeway's. You roll across the pavement, giving yourself directions.

You soon arrive. You enter through the backyard. Nellie, the family dog, knows you and can talk to you. She's seen you in Janway's room.

"What are you doing here?" she asks. You tell her your story. She offers you a ride to Janeway's room. You thank her and accept. Once in Janeway's room, you lay yourself on her bed. Janeway enters her room. When she sees you, unlike at school, she bursts into tears of joy. She puts you back in your glass case. It's still very stuffy in there, but you don't mind. You're glad to be home.

Worthless

EMMA BERNSTEIN ✳ *age 11*
Brandeis Hillel Day School

I nestle into the girl's pocket, feeling the wind brush against my cold, metallic surface. I feel the motion of her bike.

"Forward, forward, forward," whisper the gears.

"Forward, forward, forward," whisper the wheels.

The girl is twelve years old. She loves to race down the streets on her bike. I love being in her pocket as she races.

Though I always dream of being spent on something, I am content where I am, just another penny in the pocket of a twelve-year-old girl.

I am wrapped up in my thoughts when the wind comes. It is cold and strong, trying to grab me away from my girl. I hold on, telling myself that she needs me, that I must stay loyal.

The wind reaches into the pocket where I sit, breaking my protection. It pulls and tugs, and I slip onto the sidewalk with a soft clink.

The girl races on, not realizing her loss. I feel abandoned, forgotten, alone. She does not care; I used every bit of my energy to stay with the girl and help her, but she does not care. She bikes on, not even realizing that her penny is gone. It's not like she ever cared before, but I still gave her my all, only to be left behind.

I roll along the street, wanting to stop, to call to the girl and remind her of my existence, but I am just a penny. I do not control my actions. I am voiceless.

Thoughts stream through my flat, metallic brain. I want to cry. I cannot. I want to scream. I cannot. I want to close my eyes and dream about being human, but I cannot even dream. I am completely trapped in this copper shell.

Now I am on the street. A car drives by, splattering my beautiful copper surface with mud.

I fall still in the center of the street, just as night begins to overcome day in a battle of orange and purple. I notice a man on the sidewalk. His clothing is tattered. His beard is shaggy.

He needs me. Someone needs me, but he does not know that I am here to help him.

I try to yell to him, but I know that I cannot.

Slowly, he looks up and his eyes find me. He pulls himself up. I hold my breath. He stumbles over to me. His hand reaches down to pick me up. His fingers close around me. He smiles.

Next thing I know, he is scuttling down the street with me clenched in his fist. We arrive at a store. He holds me up high in the air, but the young lady behind the counter shakes her head, and I realize that I am worthless.

Besides, She'd Never Been Camping

ROSE BAILER ✳ *age 12*
St. Philip the Apostle School

It was a key, a small object used to unlock something. In this case, the key unlocked a door. But not just any door—the door to a mansion: the gleaming, heavy oak door to a large estate on the beach in Hawaii. Who would have guessed a regular key could bring a family together?

It was the first day of summer. Leah stood on her over-packed, hot pink suitcase. Why was her stupid father forcing her family to live in Hawaii for a whole summer? Did he have any idea he was ruining her life? No seeing her friends, no going to the pool every day, and even worse, no flirting with the cute boys. It would be different if they were going to Hawaii for vacation, but now Leah's dad was working there. Leah's dad was a total workaholic. He never had any time to spend with Leah or her younger brother Bo. *All he cares about is money*, Leah thought.

"Leah, Bo, get down here. We have to go now or we'll miss our flight!" their dad shouted from outside. "The cab is here."

"Okay, Dad. I'm coming," Leah shouted, and five minutes later Leah, Bo, and Tom were cramped in a small, smelly taxi.

"Isn't this great?" said Tom enthusiastically. "We're going to have so much fun bonding with each other. I mean, I feel guilty, ever since Mom left I haven't been doing things with you. And now, look at us, we're on our way to an adventure."

"Yeah." Leah sighed. "Hawaii is a long way from Massachusetts."

Two hours later, the Miskin family was safely on the flight to Hawaii, but the plane ride was terrible. Bo, who was sitting behind Leah, kept kicking the back of her seat, shouting, "Look out the window! Look at the clouds! Leah, we're flying, we're birds!" Leah felt like pushing him out of the airplane. She knew their parents splitting up had been hard for him, and after all, he was only seven.

The flight was torture, and the drive to their house wasn't much better in Leah's opinion. Bo was asleep next to her, drool dripping down his chin, but the worst part was her dad. Tom talked about the things their family was going to do in Hawaii, like snorkeling and surfing. To Leah, the luaus sounded like a nightmare. Finally, she just snapped.

"Dad, we all know you're going to be locked up in your office working, so stop pretending we're going to have a good time."

Tom stared back at her in shock. "I'm sorry you feel that way, Leah," he murmured. He was quiet the rest of the drive. The estate was huge. Bo stared up at it in awe. The house was a festive yellow with a huge driveway and garden. It was also right off the beach.

The family approached the large manor. Tom reached into his pocket for the key and gasped in horror as his finger stuck through his pant pocket. "Oh no," he exclaimed. "The key! The key fell out of my pocket. I've lost the key! I remember having it on the airplane and...um, no this can't be happening. I have to get inside the house. I have to work in the office. I have to print out important documents."

Tom looked up in terror. He was pale. Leah shrugged. "Just call a locksmith."

"Locksmith, right, good idea. I'll call a locksmith."

Leah and Bo decided to go swimming while their father talked on the phone. When they returned an hour later, Tom looked worse than before.

"The locksmith is closed and the nearest one is a five-hour car ride away."

"I have an idea," explained Bo, "we can camp out."

"It's the only plan we've got," Leah added.

"Okay," said Tom. "I'll get the tent and some dinner."

The family sat around a small grill ablaze with fire, holding marshmallows over it, singing, and actually not getting on each other's nerves. That night they lay in a small tent laughing about that wonderful night. In the middle of the night, Leah got up to look at the stars. She stepped out on the soft grass, took a step, and her foot landed on something hard. "A key," Leah whispered. She slipped it in the pocket of her pajama pants. She knew her dad had to work, but a few more nights in a tent couldn't hurt. Besides, Leah thought, she'd never been camping.

I'm a Penny

ELLA BOYD-WONG ✳ *age 12*
Creative Arts Charter School

I'm a penny. Penelope Penny, if you like. Tim-Tim, my favorite owner, decided I was worthless when he was twelve. Tim-Tim used to keep me in a jar, a single penny surrounded by eight snobby quarters, you-wanna-piece-of-me dimes, and understanding nickels. Over time, Tim-Tim used all the other coins, so I was left at the bottom of the jar. When Tim-Tim moved (to Boston, I think) he dumped me out of the jar, and I rolled into a crack in the floorboards. It was hot in there, and that was kind of weird for a floorboard crack. Why was it hot down there?

I found a few other pennies: my cousin Ferdinand, for instance, who was lost three years ago when Tim-Tim spilled the jar. After a while I decided it was unfair that I was stuck, so I pushed myself out. Someone else lived in the house now. It didn't smell like Tim-Tim's mom's chocolate cookies anymore.

By the time I was on the street—the cold, hard, dirty, concrete street—it was nighttime. I was tired. Do pennies get tired? I had never been tired before, but I had never seen full nighttime before, either. I set my Abe side down and bid the valiant Honest Abe good night. (He only grinned in reply.) I went to sleep.

The Missing Gold Necklace

SANTIAGO DELGADO ✷ *age 11*
Monroe Elementary School

One day, in a fine city, the richest person in the world, Jon, was on the way to an airport—or, should I say, *his* airport. He had his own airport, but really he owned almost everything. He was really nervous because he was on his way to England to attend a birthday party for the queen. He was always invited everywhere. For a gift he was taking her a gold necklace. It was beautiful, the right size, and it was secured in a very strong glass case.

When the airplane took off, he went into his room and watched TV. His plane had three floors, and in a part of the first floor was his house. He had three servants and everything he could have imagined. When the airplane landed, he just stood up and looked back into his room, then went back in and got his phone and the necklace.

When he got to the last door of the airport, it opened and there were a lot of reporters, rich people, poor people, and everyone in the city. The entire city was there when he got to his limo. He had to be followed by military troops. When he got to the palace and looked for the necklace, it wasn't there.

He was very mad. Suddenly the doors of the palace opened. It was too late to go back. So he just went into his back seat, got a big case, and went into the palace and gave the case to the queen. He was too busy, so he told her the truth, that he had to go, and he left.

Jon is one hundred years old, and, until this day, no one knows what happened.

When author Lisa Brown suggested to us that she'd like to do a workshop where students learn to write like dead people, we got all set to exhume bodies. It seemed macabre—not to mention 100 percent illegal—but we love Lisa, so we reluctantly agreed to help. Just as we were nervously about to head out to the grave-yard, the students came running to correct us: no bodies were needed. Instead, they examined old photographs (phew!) to make up strange and wonderful back-stories for the long-dead people in them, and channeled that person's voice into a letter. Sure the stories are great, but what are we going to do with all of these shovels? *

A Page from the Grave

Grave

How to Write Like a Dead Person

Audrey H. Winters

KATE IIDA ✳ *age 14*
Cascade Canyon School

MAY 26, 1907

Dear Louis,

Mother is getting worse. Today she spent the day lying in bed, staring at the ceiling and moaning as if her heart would break. Sometime later she started rocking in bed, shaking her head and muttering, "No, no, I cannot come, no, I mustn't." I must confess, after about an hour of this behavior, with her voice increasing in volume and becoming almost like a shriek, I fled from her room, being terrified that she would lash out at me as she does in her bad moods. Once, while I was tending the fire near her bed in winter, stoking it to keep her warm, her thin and emaciated hand reached out and grabbed me, pulled me in close to her so that I could see her deranged face. Louis, I thought it was the hand of death. She then spoke, in a deep, raspy voice, whispering, "Give it to me, give it now." When I asked what she wanted, she responded only with, "Now, now, before it's too late." She paused, then said, "Flee, Angelina, you must go, for it is not safe anymore! Run, run!" At this point I detached myself from her and, I am sad to say, bolted from the room, being fearful that she had left me and departed into another realm. I thought she was speaking from the dead. I am now hidden in a small cupboard under the stairs, which is too small for my mother to fit in and has become my sanctuary these past days. I keep all my drawings down here, my canvases just waiting to have paint applied to them, to have color give life to them. But I have not painted in the last few weeks because of mother's worsening condition, and my fingers itch of wanting to pick up my pen and begin to draw again.

Louis, I have been missing you so much. I wish you were here, and I feel so awful that I could do nothing to stop your father sending you to West Point. How is it there? Is it the nightmare that you anticipated? I do hope that they are allowing you to paint, for I know how much you could not stand to be separated from your paintbrushes and canvases. I am sure you shall be a great painter one day, and I hope that sometime, somewhere, I shall find you again. Perhaps we shall both be artists—with hundreds of dollars and a flat all to ourselves! Oh well, I can dream at least.

I remain your loving friend,
Audrey H. Winters

Soon to be the greatest painter this side of the Atlantic Ocean! (Along with you, of course).

* * *

MAY 27, 1907
Dear Louis,

Oh God, my hand can hardly stop shaking for sadness and grief. What have I done? Please forgive me if I seem to jump about and forgive the ink splotches made by my trembling hand—I just cannot contain myself any longer. Although it pains me to put this in writing, it must be spoken, for there is nothing else to do. My mother, loving and sainted, but also beastly and terrifying, is dead.

Beastly and terrifying! Did I just write that? Did my hand just spell out those two words about my own dear mother? It is true that near the end she did scare me with her ranting and her screaming, but why did I not pay more attention to her, even in the darkest of times, why did I not attend to her? Alas, that is the fate of those who live after those they loved have died.

Louis, I must tell you that I will not be staying here much longer. I have plans, plans that will take me far from this beastly place, where I have lived out my precious fourteen years. I am getting out, to go I know not where. May the path take me where it will, but of one thing I am absolutely certain—I am leaving today.

I have cut and sold my hair and have used it to buy passage to New York. Who knows what I shall find there, only that I will be looking for some sort of instructor or person for whom I shall work using my painting abilities. In a way, this is a bit of an escape for me; I shall finally be able to do what I like with my life.

Although I may never see you again, please remember me in your heart. I am sure I shall always remember what a great friend you were for me even in my darkest times. I feel sad that I must leave, but there is nothing to be done, and I must make my own way in this world.

Farewell, I am forever yours,
Audrey H. Winters.

Jack

JULIA MOORE ✳ *age 12*
Live Oak School

White hair that sticks out in every direction. Skin so pale it is like a blank piece of paper held up to the light. Friendly eyes, coal-black and always crinkled by his warm smile. Always cheerful. Always trusting. This was my friend, Nicholas IV, the first ringmaster.

I saw him before he died, you know. They knew I was his favorite. The clowns led me into his room just five minutes before his breathing ceased. Even on his deathbed, he managed to make that same smile. It was a smile that made everything else seem unimportant. It was that smile that was my last view of him as I was tugged out of the lamplit room.

The ringmaster died yesterday night. I was standing in my stall, straw lying around my hooves. I heard a shout from the castle-like tent. About ten minutes later, Luca and Dan staggered out of the tent, a long, slender black box resting on their shoulders. The two acrobats stumbled along. I watched until they were out of sight.

The funeral was today. Everyone was there, even me and Whisper, the circus horse. The clowns painted our red noses a sorrowful black. Figaro the Storyman was wearing, instead of a fake fur cloak, a suit and tie. Even the slapstick was at a minimum. This was a sad, sad day for the circus. The ring-master, the stone pillar that held all of us upright, was gone. Circus MideVilla was falling apart at the seams, and no one was there to stop it.

The cold rain pelted my dappled gray coat, running down my flanks, trickling through my mane. A few clowns shuttled sorrowfully out, the last stragglers of a once great circus. This was the day of the sale. Even now the word sticks in my thoughts. A rough hand gripped the damp rope halter tied on my head and tugged me toward the ring. I strained back; this was not a place I wanted to go. A crop flashed in the grey sky and a jolt of pain slashed on my side. I shot forward and reared, one of my flint-like hooves slicing my holder's arm. A few muffled curses reached my ears, but it made no difference. I was bucking and rearing, my eyes rolling, wide with fear, anything to be free. But to no avail. I was dragged forward. Into the ring. I stood alone. Wrought-iron fences surrounded me and enclosed me in their covered grip. The shouts and jeers of the crowd blurred together in a stream of words. A voice called out above the others, "Circus horse. Name of Jack. Dappled grey, strong and healthy. Let's start at fifty-thousand dollars." More shouts and jitter. I stomped my foot, trying to drown out the noise of the crowd with noise of my own. A hammer banged on a block of wood. "Sold, to the gentleman in the white coat, for seventy-five-thousand." My new owner was a scrawny-looking man with curly black hair and eyes the color of coffee. He loaded me into a trailer and drove me to a sea of pink-and-white-striped tents. A dying neon sign hung, flickering, on the largest of the tents. It read BIG TOP CIRCUS in orange letters.

Albert Daruent

ZELLA BLACKKETTER ✳ *age 12*
James Lick Middle School

Dearest Albert,

O! How we all miss you! You shall be pleased to know how
your sister is faring: much recovered from the fever of last
week. Since you have gone to the city, she doesn't quite know
what to do with herself, and I must confess my feelings are
rather similar. Yesterday—and I am sure you will laugh to read
this—as we had just hung up the washing to dry, after your
sister had tripped and dropped the clothes in the ditch for the
third time, it began to rain and Georgina ran inside, leaving
me to slosh through the mud alone.

I have heard about your financial situation from Mrs.
Wilkins, who visited from town just yesterday, and I am quite
worried and surprised. If my information is correct, you have
not had a job for a very long time. I know that since you were
eleven you have wanted to be a groomsman, and I urge you to
follow this dream.

I have also heard from Mrs. Wilkins that you have acquired
a pet snake, causing Felicity to break off your engagement.
Because you would not get rid of it? Poor, sweet girl. I do not

blame her. You should get rid of the horrid creature at once—horses will not like a person who smells of snake.

Know that we love and miss you and—please!—write back soon.

Your loving mother

✱✱✱

Brother—

Albert, I miss you so very much. I am working to make this letter look as beautiful as my teacher would like—see how my penmanship has improved! I am doing my best in school, just as you told me to before leaving, which brings me to another point. I am quite angry with you for leaving me here with our horrid brothers. They have been more tormenting than usual, pulling pranks and my hair mercilessly.

When are you going to visit?! Please, make it soon, so you can tell me all about the city and what you are doing. Mother has promised to include this letter with hers, so I must hurry up and finish. She intends to send them by the evening post. Please do write back soon!

Your loving sister,
Georgina

Albert Wolfgang

OLIVIA SCOTT ✳ *age 13*
Everett Middle School

DECEMBER 15, 1843

I don't believe birthdays are to celebrate. The only gift I received was a cold, unfriendly letter from my friend saying how much money he needs from me to buy himself a new pair of shoes. The cake I had was an old, stale cookie I found in the back of my empty, cobwebby cupboard. My dog went without food. Poor Rascal, his ribs protrude from his sides like my nose from my face. More importantly, my hair is inches longer, my face more wrinkly, and my body a year older. Really, birthdays only celebrate surviving another hard, tiresome, torturous, and annoying year of life. All that work just to survive! Who are we? Why do want we want to survive this wearisome life? If you asked me, I would give life a different name. Something more prominent, something longer, something more torturous, and more like life itself.

Later today I went into the park to try to drown out the bad and evil happenings of earlier. The animals were all deep in their holes, hiding away from the snow blanketing the ground, even though that most need some food. On trudging home, I walked silently past a bookstore and saw my greatest work on the shelf. Fear welled up in my soul and I picked up my pace.

For the rest of the day I hibernated in my house like the other animals. A wonderful birthday.

✳✳✳

DECEMBER 16, 1843

My friend actually visited me today. Together we went on a walk, chatting as if we were normal friends when we just happened to pass by a shoe store. In we went and the most expensive shoes were picked out. Like a good friend I bought them for him, and, as gullible as I am, believed he would pay me back. Maybe, since I believe I have earned my friend's qualities, I can write what I think about him, and he will find this journal.

Speaking of dead things—there's been a lot of talk recently about the death of the newspaper. We honestly don't understand the fuss. Our in-house newspaper, the *Valencia Bay-farer*, continues to thrive. Maybe it's because the *Bay-farer*, led fearlessly by Programs Coordinator Miranda Tsang, is where you can find top-of-the-line journalism written by eight- to fourteen-year-olds. Seriously, the newspaper world should take note. With stories on cryptozoology, *Skymall*, "the deal with dogs," and even the solitary pleasures of reading, the *Valencia Bay-farer* is filled with journalism unlike any you've ever seen. Unless, of course, you've seen the *Bay-farer* before. In which case, you win this round. ✳

Valencia Bay-farer

826 Valencia's In-House Newspaper

SkyMall: The Essence of Insanity?

MIRA CHATTERJEE ✳ *Age 12*
Convent Elementry School

Imagine that you are on an arduous plane ride. You're confined to a small seat with anywhere from one to sixteen hours to kill. And you're almost definitely next to a window, aisle, or stranger. While airplanes have done their best to entertain us fliers with individual television screens, complimentary refreshments, and free food, the fact remains that there are certain times during a flight where you are unable to take a stroll around the plane or watch television on the little screens. The fifteen minutes either taking off or landing are an excellent time to browse through the numerous collections of safety and shopping magazines alike. One of the best sellers is the infamous *SkyMall* magazine, an in-flight and online shop that sells a variety of somewhat random products.

Some of SkyMall's most memorable products include the Nuclear Globe (picture a giant spotted hamster ball specifically designed for the pool, which happens to be $400), the discreet 2GB pen (a $90 pen that has the handy and completely useful plus of being able to record video), and the inflatable turkey (made of "completely inedible vinyl" according to *skymall.com*). There are also the nifty security and safety products; the most interesting include the Wireless Color Mirror camera (a $500 dollar video camera disguised as a mirror) and the Evac Fire Escape Hood (don't ask, just look at the picture). In 2009, some of the top sellers included the Keep Your Distance Bug Vacuum (a clever device which has the ability to suck up flying insects from up to two feet away) and the Pet Observation Porthole (a plastic viewing bubble for your pet to "give your inquisitive canine a panoramic view of the world.") The latter was actually popular enough to sell out in 2009.

However, SkyMall's products aren't all as goofy and laughable as they may seem. In an interview with the *New York Times*, Christine Aguilera, the president of *SkyMall*, says, "Some may think that what we provide is just a good laugh. There's nothing wrong with that. But when you are standing eye to eye with a giant spider, you will be thankful you bought the Keep Your Distance Bug Vacuum." Bill McKibbin, who wrote an article in the cultural and artistic *Orion Magazine*, says, "If there's any piece of writing that defines our culture, I submit it's the *SkyMall* magazine. To browse its pages is to understand the essential secret of American consumer life: that we've officially run out—not only of things we need—but even of things we might plausibly desire."

Seafood Watch— How Important Is It Really?

HANA O'NEILL * *Age 13*
St. Stephen School

The Monterey Bay Aquarium's Sustainable Seafood Program—Seafood Watch—can make a huge difference if everyone makes an effort. Much of the seafood that we eat is farmed or caught in ways that harm the environment. The Seafood Watch Program is trying to increase the percentage of the seafood we eat that does not harm the Earth.

The mission of the Monterey Bay Aquarium is to inspire conservation of the oceans. Their Seafood Watch Program, which has been around since 1999, is one way they are seeking to do this. The program "seeks to raise conservation awareness among seafood consumers and transform the seafood market so that commercial incentives favor sustainable fisheries and fish-farming practices" (from the Aquarium's *Research and Conservation Report 2010*). The Aquarium recently came out with a Seafood Watch app for iPhones. It is free and has been downloaded more than five hundred thousand times. Also, more than 37 million pocket guides have been distributed. These pocket guides are updated frequently—every six months—because new discoveries are always being made. You can download the iPhone app or a PDF of the pocket guide, both for free, at *seafoodwatch.org*.

While the pocket guides are helpful and will make a difference, the iPhone app is much more helpful. Pocket guides are updated, but people are not always aware of this. However, new discoveries are sent automatically to the iPhone. Also on the iPhone is the Project Fish Map. On this feature, users can mark places where the food they ate was sustainable. This will become more and more useful as more and more locations get tagged as sustainable.

At the Monterey Bay Aquarium, there is an exhibit called the Real-Cost Café that provides information about some good and bad choices for our environment. There are seven or eight "bar" seats, and each has an electronic menu set up in front of it. You have three choices for "entrées," and each person picks what they want. Then a chef and two waiters, on video screens set up in front of a bar, give you facts about how your "meal" was raised. At the end, you receive a "Guest Check" that tells you how high a cost this type of seafood has on the environment. I found this very, very interesting, and it really made me think about the huge impact our eating has on the animals I like—for example, sea turtles and sea otters—and the ones that most people are scared of, like sharks. Sharks are on the "avoid" side of the pocket guide.

Alison Barratt, the Communications Senior Associate Manager at the Aquarium, says, "The Real-Cost Café was our first exhibit attempt to integrate humor with a serious message. We wanted to put people in a realistic setting— choosing from a menu at a dinner and finding out what the 'real cost' of their seafood is... We want people to walk away knowing that some choices are better than others when it comes to eating seafood, and that their choices can really make a difference." That's similar to how I felt leaving the Café a couple of weeks ago. I felt like I should be very careful about my choices from now on, because some techniques are really hurting the environment.

Other steps that the Monterey Bay Aquarium is taking to spread the message of being eco-friendly include interactive activities in the Aquarium and on the website. One of the activities at the Aquarium is located outside the "Hot Pink Flamingos" exhibit. It is an activity where people choose a pledge to help the environment, take a picture of themselves, and watch theirs and other people's videos on a big screen. This is just one example of many.

Two things you could do to help our oceans are to download the app or the pocket guide (and use it), and tell your friends about this program. If you get your friends and family to watch what they eat, they will start to tell more people, who will tell other people, who will tell even more people. The more people that make ocean-friendly choices, the bigger difference this Seafood Watch Program will make. If we all gave this our all, we could really make a huge difference. But we have to do it together. We can't do it alone.

How to Avoid a Shark Attack

WILDER WINDELER * *Age 9*
Marshall Elementary School

Did you know that sharks don't mean to attack humans? They just think the bottom of the surfboard is a seal's belly. Recently, a shark killed a sixteen-year-old South African. According to the *LA Times*, the species of shark was unknown. The shark attack happened January 17, 2011 at Second Beach, Port St. Johns, on the Eastern Cape of South Africa.

These are some tips to avoid shark attacks: always swim in a group; don't wander off too far from shore; avoid waters at night, dawn, or dusk; don't enter the water if bleeding; don't wear shiny jewelry; don't go into waters containing sewage; and don't relax just because porpoises are nearby.

These tips should save you from shark attacks.

Doodling Does a Body Good

RUBY NICOLE SMITH ✳ *age 10*
Alvarado Elementary School

Most people think doodles are just little time-wasting pictures that make people unfocused. But doodling actually helps you stay focused and stops you from daydreaming.

It can also give you better art skills. Also, big companies use doodles; Google has they're own doodlers to do doodles to make out the letters of Google. Many people consider doodles respectable artwork (which it is). It can also lead to creative artwork because it's a lot like practicing. Doodling is also helpful because there is no age you have to be to start doodling. Another cool thing about doodling is that it can actually say things about you, and gender can affect your doodling. Doodling is important, and there are interviews to prove it.

Doodling is not like most people think: a waste of time. Doodling helps you pay attention and not daydream. This is how it works: daydreaming takes a ton of brain power, more than you thought. You will begin, then you will think about where you are going to go on the trip, and pretty soon you will practically be on the trip itself. But if you doodle, you will stay in your whole body, not just your head. A *Time Magazine* study, "Doodling Helps You Pay Attention," says, "Before the tape began, half the study participants were asked to shade in some squares and circles on a piece of paper. They were told to not worry about being neat." They also said, "The doodlers creamed the non-doodlers: on tape, those from the doodlers who recalled 7.5 pieces of information (out of 16 total) were on an average 29 percent more than the average of 5.8 recalled by the control group."

One very important thing about doodling is that it is not the same thing as drawing. Because drawing you really think about, and doodling is just happy little pictures where you hardly think at all, and you just do it. "You think about drawing, doodling you just do," said Roland Smith.

Yet another important thing about doodling is that you can do it at any age. You can start at as young as one and never stop doing it. "Two," answer Isabel Hansen after I had asked her when she started doodling. There are a few similar things people doodle on. These things are folders, classwork, homework, and binders. "Schoolwork, paper, folders, and binders," said Roland Smith.

Doodling can actually say things about who you are. For instance, a study from *The Register* interviewed Dr. Burns. In the article, Dr. Burns says, "For example a commonly drawn doodle is a tree. Trees represent growth and life." Another part of this article asks, "Do men and women doodle differently?" The answer is yes. Dr. Burns yet again can prove it: "Men tend to doodle geometric shapes while women are more likely to doodle human figures and faces." That is what doodling says about you and how gender affects it.

Now let's be honest, doodling isn't always good. Sometimes teachers get angry, you run out of time on your math or other work because you are doodling, and other times people get so wrapped up in doodling that they forget to work. Sarah Kirby-Smidt says, "Mr. Guzman yells at me to stop."

There are (even though you probably don't think so) professional doodlers, such as the people who doodle for

Google. Also Shaun, a master-doodler/dark artist who does his art with dark pencil. There are most likely others, but that is another article.

Doodling will maybe someday become a strategy for daydreamers that teachers and scientists recommend and encourage, but that day hasn't come yet. Maybe doodling will someday become a very encouraged thing for young artists to practice. But these things are all for a different article. Because right now all scientists and I know is that it can help you concentrate. I hope you learned something new about doodling that you didn't know, but who knows, there could be more you don't know.

Not Your Regular Mermaid Article

AVA LYNCH ✳ *Age 10*
St. Anne's School

If you think this is one of those regular articles about mermaids, then you really shouldn't read this at all, because this is about different kinds of characteristics of mermaids and where those characteristics came from.

Some people may think mermaids are real, but other people (like my uncle) do not. If you believe in mermaids, you are probably wrong, because nobody has ever seen a mermaid, and nobody knows how mermaids give birth or what they eat.

Mermaids originally came from Greek mythology, but some stories may not be true. According to the New World Encyclopedia, some sailors may have confused mermaids with manatees because manatees hold their young the same way mermaids hold their young. Also, sailors might have been confused by the way manatees' tails are shaped just like mermaids' tails. In mythology, mermaids like music, and sometimes sailors were lured to their deaths by their beautiful voices. But mermaids have may been confused with sirens,

THE *826 QUARTERLY* * VOL. 14

even though sirens are half-human, half-bird instead of half- human, half-fish.

Well, you basically got all the facts out of me about mermaids. So I guess this is the end.

Half a miracle is a difficult thing to be. It's like you can cure someone of blindness, but only enough to make them painfully near-sighted. Or keep them from falling off a bike, only to have them ride all day and get a sunburn. Perhaps that's too negative a way to look at it. If something is half a miracle, it could be the necessary thing that needs to be there for a miracle to happen. Like, you can't make a carpet fly if you don't have a carpet. Make sense? No? Maybe this will help. In this collection of bilingual poetry by students at James Lick Middle School there are all sorts of half miracles, and even a couple full-on ones. ✳

Half a Miracle

Seventh-Grade Poetry from James Lick Middle School

My Library

MIREYA PEREZ * *Age 11*
James Lick Middle School

My family is a library.
My mom is a scrapbook
full of memories and bits of burritos from her work.
My dad is an encyclopedia,
knowing so many things, like Japanese
and how to cook pasta.
My little brother is a picture book,
not explaining or understanding words.
My older brother is a lost book,
never returned to our library or to this world.
And me—
I am a diary—
containing secrets
and only opening
with a key.

2030

CHASE LOUIE ✳ *Age 12*
James Lick Middle School

In 2030 I'll die from rabies.
I'll turn into a ghost
and eat some red cherries.
I'll go and spook out the creators
of Sesame Street.
I'll go into my enemy's house
and kick his feet.
Next time I see him
I'll kick his feet.
Maybe I will have my own
ghostly husky and name him Cody.
I will even pull
pranks on Justin Bieber because he sings like a girl.
I'm going to visit France
and follow some mimes.
I will spy on the
clerks in a bank when they open the safe.
I will then send a
secret message to my parents telling them the code so
    they'll be
rich.
During my
ghostly life, I will live in a mansion full of other ghosts.
So I won't
be lonely.

Ode to a Doughnut

JONATHAN RIVERA ✳ *Age 12*
James Lick Middle School

Oh beautiful, sugary, round doughnut.

My savory lifesaver.

Color brown soft bread.

Born of the baker. You make everyone
happy with your deliciousness. When the
doughnut is gone,

it feels like your family is not with
you. When I eat a doughnut, it feels like

I got all A's in school. I opened a half
of a miracle

drifted from a doughnut store.

Baseball Stadium

RIKI DIAZ PEREZ ✳ *Age 11*
James Lick Middle School

My baby brother is the field.
I'm the seat.
My big brother is the lights.
My mom is the doors.
My dad is the outside.
And the baseball players tickle
my baby brother.
I hear people cheering
when baseball players
make a home run. And my
big brother turns different-colored lights.
My dad can just hear
the loud noise.
The game finishes and
my mom
shuts the doors.

Ode to My Fuzzy Socks

FEBE GONZALEZ ✳ *Age 12*
James Lick Middle School

Ode to my fuzzy socks—
the softy bag on my feet,
the feeling on the floor,
the whole world is my
socks.

Sad

ANGELI SANTIAGUEL ✳ *Age 12*
James Lick Middle School

Sad looks like a huge tidal wave trying to bowl you over.

Sad feels like holding an empty eggshell.

Sad smells like a toxic dumpster, like a landfill that doesn't
love you.

Sad tastes like an onion, like a baby whining on the floor.

Sad sounds like a tire deflating in the middle of nowhere.

My Whale House

SERGIO BECERRA PARRA * *Age 11*
James Lick Middle School

In 2030...

I will be thirty years old.

I will live in the Pacific Ocean.

I will talk to Aquaman
about a house.

My house will be

inside a whale. It will
have internal organs as
furniture.
And seeing stuff in its eyes,
I will take a bath

in the blood of the whale.

I will shoot water out
of cannons.
I will have an army
of sharks
to conquer

other whales.

I'm going to conquer
the Seven Seas and Poseidon's
Throne.

I will put army men
all over the city to
protect my people.

Wierdos

KIRA ESCOBAR ✳ *Age 12*
James Lick Middle School

My house is full of weirdos.
My dad is the guy in the straitjacket.
My mom is Dracula's cold-blooded helper.
My cat is wanted in Turkey.
My dog is a goat that will eat my hand.
I am a peacock-tail-eating,
trampoline-jumping crazy person.

Furious

PATRICK RODIL ✳ *Age 12*
James Lick Middle School

Furious looks like
a volcano trying to
explode with a meteor
that is dodging the lava.

Furious feels like a
snake ejecting white,
slimy poison into my
body that bubbles up
every time I take
a breath in.

Furious smells like
rotten bones that were
burned by Hell's ashes,
destroying my soul.
Furious tastes like
rough steak with
bitter bones made
from dead souls
that were never found by
their owners.

Furious sounds like
spirits laughing crazily
and sobbing and weeping,
being tortured by

Hades's warriors saying,
"Your soul will
be gone, so
get out!"

Writing and Publishing Apprentices is a year-round workshop designed to guide whatever creative writing projects students have in mind. Whether they're working on poetry, lyrics, comics, creative nonfiction, or something in between, students in this class receive guidance from adults who write and edit for a living. The class is coordinated by 826 Valencia Publishing Director Justin Carder and is made up of middle-and high school students from all over the Bay Area—who are all really cool, by the way. Cooler than us. A couple of them even came in for the editorial board of this very book. If that's not cool, then tell us: What is? No, seriously. Tell us. ✲

Babies and the Metric System

Selections from Writing and Publishing Apprentices

Adrian

PAOLO YUMOL ✶ *Age 16*
Lick-Wilmerding High School

Adrian tells her about how he is taking medication to keep
him from becoming a turnip.

"It's true," he says. He removes from his pocket an orange
capsule filled with pills, which he dangles in front of her like
a bell. Carmen laughs. And with her shoulders, too. He wishes
it was all that easy and decisive, pure science: he rings the bell
and the dog comes running for food. Pavlov, the turnip. "I was
widening at the waist and getting pinker by the minute.
Something had to be done."

"A round life it must be, the life of a turnip." She laughs.

"Naturally," he says. "But out of all the things you'd expect
out of turning into a turnip, no one ever salivated for me. You'd
think dogs on the street, or small children even, smacking their
lips. But no. Nobody ever salivated for me."

"Really," she says. "Somehow, I find that hard to believe."

This makes Adrian flutter like he hasn't fluttered in months.
They are talking during her break, edging on the end to another
slow day, snow creeping up the thighs. She has already taken
off her apron and has been ignoring customers, brewing a
little sluggishly. Not Adrian, though. Adrian brews like a
sociopath.

"You live close, don't you?" she says. "I'll walk you to your apartment after we close up." Adrian swallows very hard.

They give up at 8p.m. and lock the door behind them, burrowing into the white-walled trenches that line the sidewalk.

"I heard your house was emptied out," she eases in.

"Like a suitcase," he says.

"That's terrible," she says, though smirking, as if in response to a joke that really wasn't all that funny. "I hope you didn't deserve it, whatever it was."

"I might have." Adrian shrugs. "I'm a jerk."

"Jerk or not," she grins. "I want to know what happened to you."

* * *

They came in and took all his stuff. The three of them, sagging on the sidewalk in front of his stoop, their stained shirts, with their baseball caps, their bodies a lazily penned ellipsis that slumped blank and unimpressive against the fast traffic. One by one they squeezed through his doorway, miserly extracting every single piece of furniture from the house like a drop of blood from his veins.

Collateral, they called it. If I had things my way, your head on a silver platter would be collateral, you swines.

Then they drove away and Adrian stood helpless as his previous life packed itself up and skipped town, without even a note. Insane.

He entered his house, nothing but skeletal remains now, boxing him in walls of silence, like an oversized terrarium. A mausoleum. And when he found that single turnip, sitting inside his cupboard, looking a lot like a thumb, radiating that stupid, purple-red hue like a grin, he knew he was going to lose it. He set it in the center of the room, meaningfully, and started to cry.

* * *

They stumbled through the snow, betraying the rigid sobriety of the vast whiteness marking their path, which they stamp out like candles under each footstep. "This turnip thing," she says. "What is it, exactly? Is it 'you are what you eat,' only gone terribly wrong?"

"Less than that," he says. Adrian realizes that every woman he's ever dated, every woman he's ever known, has been an iteration of Carmen; she's appeared to him over and over again, in different shapes and sizes, like a disguised goddess, testing him. For this Adrian feels very worthy. "It's something both very animal and very vegetable, let's leave it at that." They are standing above an underpass. The feeling of the turnip growing inside of him, that fluid pulse, the second heartbeat, has slowed.

"That's so strange," she says. "You're so strange."

"I belong laid out on a table somewhere, somewhere I can get tested, where doctors and scientists can examine me."

"It's alright."

"What if I end up in a museum? Or worse, a traveling carnival, to be passed around like a comic book?"

"Adrian." She kisses him, and Adrian doesn't know what to do with hands, so he tucks them into his jacket and doesn't care if he ever sees them again.

* * *

It was going to get a lot worse before it got any better. After a consecutive week of being alone with the turnip, things were beginning to get tribal for Adrian; he found himself, one afternoon, with his stomach on the floor, clumsily and so unbeautifully not-arched, like a beached whale, peering over the turnip, which screamed its purple hue against the walls like a strobe light. This had been going on for the past few days, where Adrian would peer over the turnip as religiously as people everywhere else watched their television sets, going for days without eating.

When he took his first few steps out of the house for seven consecutive foodless days, Adrian felt, at first, fine. Peachy, even. He sighed and clucked his tongue as if things had been just as peachy for a long time. Then he heard a fat sound. The fat sound was a low and heavy note, as if someone had learned against the far left side of a piano. Then the note began to rise and fall, to the tune of a slow, pensive jig, something that sounded to Adrian maybe German or Italian in timbre and tone.

He couldn't get it out of his head. He retained the turnip's song like a bruise, a dent in his skull that owed itself to a war injury or a visit straight to the linoleum as a baby. And after his mind went, his body fell like dominoes. He began to stretch in all these different directions, taking the turnip's shape with his entire body, imitation as the sincerest form of flattery.

He gave up on frantic philosophy—if a turnip falls over in an empty house, does it make a sound?—and instead embraced the weary odd logic of the sleep-deprived metamorphoid. If he wasn't a turnip, then what was he? Nothing worthwhile, that was for sure.

* * *

The next morning there they both are, on his floor, on top of the tarp he has been using for a bed. The turnip lies just across from him, its weight shifted in a condescending hip stance. He turns over and instead watches her breathe. Her chest, rising and falling. He puts an arm across her stomach and feels it: her heartbeat, which, eyes drifting closed, he studies like Morse code.

* * *

He went in for a physical and had his suspicions confirmed. His body was transforming, and there were X-rays and every-thing to prove it. He shouldn't feel bad about it. He was a miracle. "I'm a walking phenomenon," he said to the receptionist after leaving the doctor's office. She smiled sarcastically and sent him to the pharmacist.

∗∗∗

He is woken up again by a wrench in his gut. He feels different, as though every single skin cell is changing shape, color, texture, right beside her. He is heating up. He is expanding. He can't rely on the turnip anymore, and instead his second heartbeat extends its veins, weaves its arterial coffin, flowing canals wrapped around a bleeding continent. Adrian blooms from vegetable to organ.

∗∗∗

She isn't quite as talkative two mornings over.

She tells him one thing, though, and that's not to talk about what happened. Then silence for the rest of the morning.

The silence is so excruciating in fact that Adrian finds all the wrong words bubbling at his tongue. She rings up her twentieth customer and gives him a stony look, and he says the words, "Jeez. Who died?"

Which sends him leaving for home early, nauseous, wishing his foot could angle itself all the way around to kick his own face.

The second heartbeat grows even more urgent as he steps through his front door. He mutters under his breath. Suddenly he feels very sick. He collapses on the floorboard and pumps. He doesn't breathe or convulse; he pumps. "Watch me pump!" he shouts. He wonders if any of it is real, if flesh can really balloon that easily, if he can be a turnip one day and a walking, talking human heart the next, a pulsing freakshow. To rip open his shirt and see his chest curled like a red, clenched fist is enough to break the trance. He feels and understands the melodrama like only a human heart can.

∗∗∗

Three days before she leaves for L.A., she takes him to her apartment. There are books stacked in steep columns, framed photographs along every inch of her bookcases. There's almost nowhere for Adrian to step. His house is a silent Pangea; this apartment, her apartment, is a shattered plate of jagged continents, volcanic islands. Every square inch of the place is draped in clutter and vicious, vicious color. He is overstimulated. He feels like an addict.

"Well, this is it," she says. "I'm sorry there isn't a lot of room for you." Adrian shrivels up. The apartment is tiny, a suitcase, without any room to stretch, to expand, to breathe. He wonders how she can live like this.

"I am too."

Hamlet, You Were Wrong, Being Is Like Not Being

MEGAN MADDEN * *Age 17*
The Urban School

If only we had two souls, then I could send one of mine away to death to breathe some strength into this one. If only I could put a thumb down on the page of this world and come back to my place later if need be. But I can't, and I am tired, and I need sleep.

I am not made of the stuff from this world. It is always kill, kill, kill, a million and one earthquakes at every small turn of my internal earth. It is always having to pull your own hair from your hairbrush, spooling in concentric circles for efficiency. It used to be that we thought our hair would make a nice fairy bed. Now it's just the detritus, the runoff, the drudge and the grime, a constant reminder that the spool of thread must go on.

I used to be a lady. I was a dame, a womb, a sacred secret cave of sighs. But I know now how things go. I know the world is a series of mirrors you can't look past. I know a mirror placed parallel to a mirror casts an image that can't end. I know that everything I see is something that's already happened, something I can't touch.

Bombarded by subatomic particles all day long, participating in the weary job of the decay and regeneration of cells, constantly plagued by the screaming voice of electrical signal and interstitial fluid. Every spirit in this world is taking hold of me all at once, grasping my shoulders, and refusing to let go. No. I was not made for that. I am forlorn in my wayward body, with a heart beating like a racehorse in a state of cardiac fibrillation whenever any small shift on axis begins to take hold, with a numbing throb of predictability. And that thing, my heart, which sends tangible, life-force-bringing strings to every nook and cranny of this vessel of mine—well, it's working overtime to cocoon my sensory soul.

There is something more in keeping in what is ebbing and flowing out of that sky with what is ebbing and flowing out of me, far from what this world shoves into my crumbling organs. Something much, much closer to what they are used to knowing. Something that, with each passing moment, propels them gleefully toward the moment when they'll meet it.

Sleep, sleep, sleep, that's all we need. For what we find in this world—that is only a whisper of our former or future selves. Sometimes on wild-horse days you can hear your own musky breath calling from far above, like a preview of your own inevitable extrication from body.

Fear deters us from pursuing the only thing that might actually hold something redeeming. Perhaps we are undecided about whether to die, because there is something very like death inside us already. I am dead every time I smell the wind, and every time a hair of mine grows. And when we dream.

When we dream, we are always dead. But the thing I am always forgetting to call meaningful is that we wake up. Maybe we are dead already. Maybe we wake up in the butterflies of morning and hear the small whisper of darkness between the beatings of stationary wings. But consciousness keeps us from seeing it as so. Who said death wasn't a charge of subatomic particles anyway? To live, we hold fast to the idea of death, sharp and unmasked, our conscious sense of the underlying current of life.

Common Intruder

BO YAN JUSTINE MORAN ✳ *Age 16*
Lick-Wilmerding High School

HERA

My eyes were fogging over my fingers when we heard the smooth growl of the wheels gliding over the oil-fouled, spot-stricken cement. My hands lambasted the table; her pencil clattered; and then all were extinguished. The door shut unsurely and then was shut, the shaking silence was tapped by the hollow footsteps as he sluggishly scraped up the stairs and the once joy-ensuing tinkle prodded open the front door.

The yawn of the second glass door ran us into Alastor as he stepped into the threshold of us. Themis annexed herself to Alastor's arm, and I vacillated in the doorway as he gave me nothing in his eyes like always.

Alastor unsecured his daughter's grappling fingers from his arm; with each extricated finger, Themis's sanguine, febrile face mutated into knowing puzzlement, and my face rests in animus, at the tip of detonation.

THEMIS

I stuck my fingers on him but he picked them off one by one like not-wanted and strode past us down the stairs to their once-was peaceful-sleep, now-is-tormented respite. We moved no muscle until she did.

Alastor! Alastor! What happened to you? Where are you... are you staying? Hera yelled after him.

The whisps of their talk floated to me, as I wondered at his brown shoes' style I have never seen.

My ears hurt an awkward clangor that I padded to see Hera's semi-caught body as she gashes her shirt in half, screaming.

He pounds the rest of the way up the stairs. I race his pounding to the glass door where I ensnared it.

Move Alastor gruffed Move

Please I say Please I say Why

Because he says he splintered my back through the door. The pieces say Last time Last time Last time

He was a common then a common-intruder no-more-now intruder as the smooth growl doesn't return.

ALASTOR

I just came for my toothbrush.

Chicken Little

LUCIE PEREIRA ✳ *Age 14*
Crystal Springs Uplands School

"Okay. Okay. I'll be right home. Yeah, twenty minutes. Okay. Sounds good. Love you too. "Kay, bye." He slipped his cell phone into his coat pocket and pushed through the revolving doors, nodded to the receptionist, and gripped his briefcase in his hand. As he stepped out onto the sidewalk, he could feel his body heat leaving him and floating into the air in invisible wisps, lost to him, as he pulled his coat closer to his body.

He walked east toward the subway station, sucking in cold breaths through his mouth that chilled his insides. He ran through the necessary grocery items he needed to pick up on the way home, remembered to remind his wife to call the guy who promised that he was able to fix their impossible furnace, wondered if the kids were home from piano lessons yet. He paused in his thoughts, and that minute pause was the perfect opportunity for something extraordinary to happen.

It fell straight down and clattered to the sidewalk. He alone halted, looked up to see where it came from, bent down to pick it up. It was sky blue, flat, and about an inch thick, soft and cushiony on the outside like an old quilt. Yet it had jagged edges where it appeared to have broken off from something.

He stood up and looked around again, and he noticed. He noticed a tiny black pinprick in the blue, blue sky, so tiny he could barely detect it. He held up the object, and shivered when the color of it perfectly matched the sky above.

"The sky is falling," he murmured to nobody. Then, louder, now more convinced, "The sky is falling!"

A little girl, clutching the hand of her mother, stopped and looked at him. A young man paused long enough to aim a sad smile at him, a small sign of pity. Other than that, nobody stopped. The crowd of people gave him a wide berth, repelled like the wrong ends of two magnets. But once they got around their temporary obstacle, they were packed tightly together again. He gave one final glance upward before unbuckling his briefcase and tucking the object inside of it. Then he continued on his way.

The staircase was unassuming, just a sudden hole in the sidewalk. There were no flashing lights or large signs that said it was the subway. People disappeared down it, descending to a different level of the world, a little deeper into the earth. The blue sky disappeared from over his head, replaced by a dark, dismal gray ceiling. Everything seemed dirty underground, but he just kept walking, stopped to insert his ticket into the metal machine, and kept walking once again. He only stopped when he got on the roaring subway, sleek and loud. He kept expecting the motion of the train to make the object in his briefcase rattle, to give away some scandalous information of what he had found, until he remembered that it was soft and padded and secret. He gripped his briefcase a little tighter. At each stop, a stream of people squeezed their way through the doors of the train.

His phone, lying in his coat pocket on top of a bedding of gum wrappers and receipts, buzzed, barely detectable through the thick material of his coat. He plucked it from his pocket and flipped it open, checking his text message. It was his wife, asking where he was. According to her, he said he'd be home fifteen minutes ago. He checked his watch. He must have been standing on the sidewalk for much longer than he'd thought. It was no wonder people had begun to stare.

They arrived at his stop and he stepped off the train. He climbed the broken escalator and walked out into the sunlight. It was about five degrees warmer at his house than at his office, but it seemed like much more than that to him. The sunlight rested on his skin, a tangible presence. Pensive, he walked the three blocks from the subway station to his apartment. There was a small bench not two yards from the door of the building, old and rotting and lichen-covered. The metal legs were rusted but sturdy. He sat down on the bench and it gave a creaky greeting. It seemed to him that his weight was more of a comfort than a burden, proof that the bench was still intact enough to do its job.

He crossed his ankles and pulled his briefcase onto his lap. He undid the silver buckles, the clicking sounds that they made startling him. He had forgotten how loud they were, how sharp in comparison to the dulled sounds of the city around him.

He took out the soft blue object and felt its weight in his hands. That rational grown-up part of him in the back of his mind told him he should be doing something: contacting the scientists, the media, or the government. But those people seemed so far away and so unreal, and he didn't trust them to love the beauty of this object like he did right now, while it rested on his palms and balanced on his fingertips. At this moment he just sat and appreciated the fact that he held a piece of the sky in his hands and let the other part of his brain rule, the part that believed in magic. Time passed, the sky darkened. Stars twinkled. He watched as the sky in his hands changed with the atmosphere overhead, from light blue to navy blue to deep indigo to pure black.

Eventually, he placed his very own piece of the sky back into his briefcase, redid the silver buckles, and sat some more. The door of the apartment building swung open with a squeaky noise, and his wife walked out and came toward him, her arms wrapped around her body, her breath making a light fog in the dim night. "Honey, is that you? I saw someone on the bench from our window, but I wasn't sure...I mean...what are you doing?"

He stayed seated on the bench, quiet.

"Where have you been?"

He stood up silently, kissed her on the cheek as a hello, and stepped into the lobby, trying to get his mind to go back to his life where people had to be home on time and pieces of the sky didn't fall from the heavens.

We never looked that great in snapshots. Our eyes are always red, and we usually look kind of weird-colored. And we wonder, do we really look like that? Still, every once in a blue moon, a photograph develops that brings out our good side. Our hair looks radiant. Our teeth make that dinging sound. In the following creative pieces, the seventh-grade students in Ms. Babcock and Ms. Hacker's classes at James Lick Middle School delved into their memories to create snapshots with words. Some of those moments are like that photo in which you look surprisingly good. In others it's more of a deer-in-the-headlights sort of thing. Either way, they all end up in the shoebox under your bed. ✻

Snapshots

James Lick Middle School's Exploration into Memory

Girls

JUAN SALAZAR ROMERO ✳ *Age 13*
James Lick Middle School

I just wanted to write about girls.
I want to know more about them.
I'm curious about them.
I want to know what they like
so I can take them where they like.
But where would I take them?
We might go to a Giants game at AT&T Park.
We might go on vacation.
We could go to Brazil to the beach,
where the water is blue and the sand is brown.
We'd go swimming, and the fishes would be as bright as a
    piece of diamond.

Out the Window

JOSEFINA SABATINO ✳ *Age 13*
James Lick Middle School

I clicked the holders off and removed the screen. I cranked the handle around as the window turned open, and the moon shined into my room. I placed one leg out through my window— then the other followed with chills. First I stood on the ledge, feeling the roughness on the soles of my feet, then sitting and feeling the same roughness. It was so peaceful, this place. The ledge faced the city, whose lights were blurry in my eyes. I felt the cool, wet air brush my cheeks. I tugged my legs and feet closer to my chest to keep warm. I loved it out here, where I didn't belong, where she didn't want me to be. It felt good to be somewhere cold where I could think. On the ledge, that ledge.

Prisoners on a Boat

XIANNA RODRIGUEZ * *Age 14*
James Lick Middle School

Stuck on a boat with twenty-nine other kids. The sun was shining, the boat was rocking, and students were talking. As the captain was giving instructions to the crew, he ordered us to be silent! I was sitting next to my friend. We were giggling about something. The captain told us to be quiet, and no talking! We felt like prisoners on a boat. We had our heads down, our hands over our mouths, and we were sitting with our legs crossed. We were scared to even yawn. We felt the boat rock and the water splashing into the boat. We couldn't stand it. I looked up at the shadow of the captain and hoped the end was near.

Daymare of Dog

UCHENNA MBATA * *Age 13*
James Lick Middle School

I remember a time when I was chased by a cowardly dog. It all started while I was running with my friend. I told my friend to stay with me because I was not scared of the coward dog, but I was pretty much nervous of the dog.

My friend told me that I shouldn't be scared of the dog— that it was very friendly and it was loveable to kids. It's just that you don't look eye-to-eye fearlessly with the dog and if it's following you for fun, don't start running so fast and shake your hands, otherwise the dog will think that you're crazy.

So my friend left me to continue on, but then I saw the dog just lying down on the grass on the grass, looking at me. I just broke the first dog rule, which was not to look fearlessly at the dog. I ran as quickly as I could.

Untitled

ANNABEL LACAYO ✳ *Age 13*
James Lick Middle School

Parents away to party all day. Left at Grandma's house.
Sister, brother, uncle. Grandma's cooking, scent of food
in the atmosphere, delicious rice, beans, chicken. Playing
around with my uncle and sister was great and all. He took it
too far, grabbed me. I tripped, fell, hit my head like Humpty
Dumpty, couldn't get back up again. A cut, no, a gash, no!
A hole was in my head. The fire-colored blood seeped from
the gash in my head. Fell onto my lips with the penny smell
and taste. Screaming, yelling, screaming. Paramedics in
my face. Questions, answers, questions. In the ambulance
scared, tears. Woke up in the hospital. My head was numb.
Fell asleep in the car. Felt like I would never wake up.

475

NATALIE BRUNWIN * *Age 13*
James Lick Middle School

I used to live in a
one-bedroom
apartment.
It had an
old, old people's home with super-security.
Why? No one's going to steal an old person.
Indoors we had a plethora of orchids, ferns, purple and
    green plants.
My dad had a
blue pinky cast because of a fight with a
bicycle.
Down the block there was a
laundromat named Olga's
that looked like a deli.
The laundromat had a
big, chipping mural of a
garage filled with people.
At the apartment we had a
weird-looking landlord,
like a fat, evil Santa Claus.
Outside the window we had a
rickety fire escape,
scary, rusty, covered in orchids.
One day we got a
little TV with a surprisingly good
picture.

The Road Killer

SHALIA KAIRY ∗ *Age 12*
James Lick Middle School

When my mom was driving down the road to go to Sunnydale, there was a cat, and the cat was gold and white. The cat started to walk into the road and back to the sidewalk, but it did that a couple of times. So when the cat decided to try to go back in the road direction, my mom was very confused about what the cat was going to do, so she kept on going down the hill, and *BOOM,* we heard a big noise, and we looked out and we saw a cat in the middle of the street flapping like a fish without water. Then we just went to my sister's house, then went back up the road. Then my uncle picked it up with a plastic bag and threw it away in the close-by garbage.

Pawn Shop

ESMERALA SILIEZAR ✻ *Age 12*
James Lick Middle School

It was my aunt, three cousins, both of my brothers, and me. When I first walked into the famous pawnshop in Las Vegas, it was cold, crowded, and small. When we were inside, a worker said, "Hey guys, we are going to bring out the old man." I was very, very, very excited that I was going to meet the old man. We got to take a picture with him, too. In the picture, it was my two brothers and me. The old man was sitting down in a chair, my brothers in the back, and me on the left side.

I Think They Stole My Hamster

PABLO BARRERA * *Age 13*
James Lick Middle School

I had a small, nice hamster
whose name was Rosie.
She was smart because she once ran away.
But then we found her.
One day builders came.
They had to fix the roof.
Before the last day they came to fix the roof,
our hamster was noisy, so we left her outside
The next morning,
there was no hamster—
there were no workers.
They probably stole my hamster.
My smart, nice hamster.

During National Pet Writing Month, students from 826 Valencia's After-School Tutoring program wrote about their animal companions, both real and imaginary. They wrote stories about pet elephants and roly-polys, about the difficulties of caring for a pet, and puppies who steal iPhones from the mall. After seeing the outpouring that came from these young authors, some asked about the origin of National Pet Writing Month. Turns out, you can pretty much declare any month you want National Insert-Ridiculous-Thing Month. So we've got a full calendar coming up. Like National Turnip Writing Month and National Tuber Poetry Month. Did we say we had a bunch lined up? We meant two. ✳

It Is a Hard Job Taking Care of One

Writing from National Pet Writing Month

The Found Roly-Poly

RONALDO RODRIGUEZ * *age 6*
Rooftop Elementary School

I found a roly-poly in my yard. I made a home for her. It was made of yogurt containers. One was on the bottom and the other one was on the top. The roly-poly was dying one day but she had babies. She was dying because she had babies. She had four babies. She was happy because she had babies. The babies' names were Mr. Bossy, Mr. Cute, Mr. Rey, and Mr. Handsome.

The Adventures of Mike the Lizard

YOVANA SÁNCHEZ ∗ *age 9*
Jefferson Elementary School

My imaginary pet is a striped lizard named Mike. Mike's stripes are different colors. Mike is very bright. One day my dad found Mike in the shoebox I kept him in and he told me he was going to throw him away. I was sad because Mike is a special lizard to me. Then I got an idea.

I said, "Hey Dad, please don't throw my lizard away!"

He said, "Yes, we have to throw him away because he is too big and scary."

I told him, "But Dad, Mike is special, he has special powers."

Then we went to my room and I showed my dad what Mike could do. When my dad saw that Mike had the special power of making ice he laughed and said, "Okay, you can keep him." Then we made lemonade and used Mike's powers to make ice cubes for the lemonade.

I Used to Have a Dog

KAROLINA OCHOA ✳ *age 7*
Edison Charter Academy

I used to have a dog, and it is a hard job taking care of one. You have to feed it and take it for a walk. It used to be my responsibility.

The Adventures of the Leprechaun

SOFIA MARQUEZ * *age 8*
Jefferson Elementary School

If I had a Leprechaun for a pet I would take her to the water park because we could get wet and have fun. I would hold her in my hand on the rides so she wouldn't get stepped on. She would feel safe in my hands. After we were done riding the rides we would go get a snack and lunch. For snack we would get apple milkshakes, for lunch I would get pizza and french fries, and for the Leprechaun she would get small food and small drinks. Afterward we would talk about getting another girl Leprechaun so my Leprechaun won't be alone. We would go to the Leprechaun store and buy another Leprechaun and we would go home and play together. After that we would eat dinner and brush our teeth; the Leprechauns would use small toothbrushes. After that we would go to sleep in a big bed with two small beds that I made.

My Turtle

ALEX GOMEZ ✳ *age 8*
Alvarado Elementary School

My turtle has two ears and eats humans. He can run so fast, and he looks like a pig, and he smells like barf. He has no eyes but he can track prey with his ears.

Scooby

SAMANTHA GOMEZ ✳ *age 11*
Alvarado Elementary School

CHAPTER ONE

Scooby is my pet dog. His breed is chihuahua. My dog Scooby is really friendly. When he hears footsteps he barks to make sure it is not a bad person. When my mom was pregnant he always used to go around her stomach and put his ear on her belly. He could sense that a little baby was coming, which was really cool and amazing. When my baby sister was born, my dog Scooby barked one time. Then when my mom sat down he tried to lick my baby sister, but my mom moved the baby. I hope when my baby sister grows up she will like to play with Scooby.

CHAPTER TWO

Scooby's my dog that likes to play
Swimming and playing on muddy days
Still biting on pillows all day
Cotton all over the house today
Watery eyes so tired, alright, sleep time!
"Time for a rap or nap?"
Nap time is right alright.

CHAPTER THREE

Dear Samantha

You have been a really good owner. You take me on walks and you care for me. I really appreciate it! Every time you come home from school I get really, really happy you're here. So when you see me wag my tail that means I'm really excited for something important, like you.

Sincerely,
Scooby

CHAPTER FOUR

What do you think my pet is? He is smaller than a backpack. His color is brown and white. His eyes sparkle like crystals. He has tiny little ears that are always listening for my lovely voice singing. Its name rhymes with Kuby. The animal I was referring to was my pet dog, Scooby.

Dog Best Friend

ALEX MUÑOZ * *age 11*
Edison Charter Academy

A dog named Kripto was in space. He came to Earth
with a cat sidekick. They landed on a boy's yard. He became
friends with every person named Alex.

I Wish I Had a Pet Elephant

DEJA HILL ✳ *age 9*
Miraloma Elementary School

I wish I had a pet elephant. Her name would be Ellie. She would change color by her mood. When she is happy she would turn gray, when she's mad she'd turn red.

I would ride her to school and we would stomp to make people scared. For fun I would go to my cousin's house and go play in her pool and Ellie would pretend to be a waterfall.

She has invisible wings and we would fly and sleep on the clouds. We would also buy space clothes so we could fly to the moon. On the moon we would kick alien butt, but we would have to back for dinner. After Ellie ate her peanut soup we would go to bed in a big room.

The eighth-grade student writers from Ms. Jones's peer resource class at James Lick Middle School are on a roll. Not only did they debut the first issue of their lifestyle magazine last semester, they have put out *Slick*'s second issue before the end of the school year. Covering news from the Bay Area and beyond, the student reporters continued to bring you captivating writing about topics that matter to them. In their honor, we've been trying to get people to call us "Slick," as it seems like a good nickname. It hasn't caught on yet, though we keep writing it on our name tags. ✳

Slick Magazine

A Lifestyle Magazine
by Eighth-Graders

DREAM: The DREAM Act

EMANUEL FLORES ✳ *age 13*
James Lick Middle School

Young children come to the United States at very young ages and grow up here as immigrants. The DREAM Act was created for these children. Children who weren't born in the United States risk getting deported back to their home countries where they didn't grow up. If they are lucky and do not get deported, they still struggle without many of the benefits United States citizens receive. The DREAM Act, which stands for Development, Relief, and Education for Alien Minors, is legislation that allows children who are undocumented to receive U.S. citizenship.

In order to receive U.S. citizenship through the DREAM Act, you must have arrived in the United States under the age of sixteen, graduated from an American high school or obtained a GED, and joined the U.S. military for two years or gone to college for two years.

"The DREAM Act would affect our communities in different ways," said Carlos Sanchez, Press Advisor to Representative Nancy Pelosi. "The Hispanic community is affected. We're the community with the highest number of immigrants, and I think only positive things can come when you educate your own community." With the DREAM Act in effect, students would have the ability to make it to college and further in life.

A lot of people who are not immigrants may not care about the DREAM Act. They worry that there would be too many immigrants in this country if it passed. What is important to know, however, is that this law has really specific guidelines. "The DREAM Act is catered to students," Mr. Sanchez says. "It's been narrowly tailored so that only good things can come of it. The good things are that you have a more educated population; you have a whole class of citizens and of your community that is legal and is out of the shadows." This legislation may improve the United States because it will allow people who are educated to work in higher-paying jobs that other workers cannot do.

Many students at James Lick Middle School came here as immigrants at a young age with their parents. The DREAM Act could provide these students with a better life. Some students dream of going to college but worry that their immigration status might interfere. "It's catered to students who are trying to go on after high school to college and beyond," Sanchez said.

Unfortunately, the DREAM Act failed to pass the Senate by four votes. Obama, in the State of the Union, pretty much declared that he would make it a priority to pass the DREAM Act.

If the DREAM Act does pass this year, it would really change America.

Riots, Violence, and the Rolling Stones

LAURA QUINTERO * *age 14*
James Lick Middle School

The Rolling Stones weren't just an overnight thing. A lot changed through music during the band's duration. Not only did you have rock'n'roll, but you also had a big amount of change throughout the world. People became rebellious. Many people blamed it on the music, but without music, where would we be today? At the time, not many people accepted the change, and a lot of riots broke out.

In 1964, the Rolling Stones finally toured the United States. Not many people even knew who they were. The South is really where all the controversy started. On the band's way through the South, people called them many names. The lead guitarist Keith Richards' book *Life* mentions that they were usually called "fairies" and "girls" for having long hair. If this sounds familiar, it started a long time ago. Not only that, but the riots were huge. Half of the time, the Stones tried to get off the stage as fast as possible. In *Life*, Keith Richards writes, "They put chicken wire in front of us because of the sharpened pennies and beer bottles they flung at us—the guys that didn't like the chicks screaming at us." Yup, all that just because they didn't like their girlfriends screaming at this weird-looking band.

But, of course, not all the trouble was in the South. I'm sure you know where Haight Street is. Well, it wasn't always so peaceful. In 1969, the Stones performed at the Altamont Race Track in California, outside of San Francisco. In the sixties, Altamont was dangerous. And it wasn't the hippies' fault. It was the "security," which was really Hell's Angels. Hell's Angels was a local gang that "protected" the bands that performed on Haight-Ashbury. Many people were killed or hurt by Hell's Angels. Allen Lewites from Amoeba Records said, "I think it was a great idea gone bad to throw a free concert with the Rolling Stones, the Grateful Dead, the Flying Burrito Brothers, etc. It seemed like the old phrase, 'a few bad apples spoil the barrel,' and once the Dead suggested bringing in the Hell's Angels as security, it went downhill." Lewites explained the violence. "Meredith Hunter was murdered. Three others died accidentally. With a show that size, sometimes the body count is four or five people trampled or suffocated. But at Altamont, it was the dark side of human nature."

The Rolling Stones weren't perfect. Most of you don't even know about a band from the sixties, but come on. People were crazy about this band. If they had stuck to the Beatles' image, I'm sure that the fans would have had a heart attack. I know I would have. Not only are the Rolling Stones the best band of all time, but also their voices and experiences speak through their music. So take your time to check them out! After this, I hope you do!

Life with ADHD

ROBERTA STROMAS ✳ *age 14*
James Lick Middle School

To really get into the mind of someone who has ADHD
(Attention Deficit Hyperactivity Disorder), I interviewed a
teacher at James Lick Middle School and a student who has
ADHD. The student said that in her mind, it's like a car that
won't stop; it's going fast and she can't stop it. She said that
in school, she had a hard time in class because the teachers
didn't get how hard it was for her. She couldn't stay in one
place, and people looked at her like she was crazy.

I went to talk with the teacher to see how she teaches
students who have ADHD. She said, "I don't like talking a lot. I
give them the opportunity to move around the classroom, and
I like to play games that relate to what they are doing in class
and their daily routines." She likes giving students things for
being good. Positive spaces make learning fun. To the question of whether it is harder to teach students with ADHD, the
teacher said, "At first it was hard." Over her teaching years, it
has gotten easier. The next question was about what students
with ADHD need in order to do well in school. They need to
be interested in what they are learning, and they need time to
calm down. They need routines and assistance.

Some students take pills to help slow the ADHD down, but sometimes they don't work. Ritalin is a medication that is prescribed to treat ADHD and narcolepsy. Although it is a stimulant that helps people with narcolepsy stay awake and alert, it can also affect certain chemicals in the brain to produce a calming effect in people with ADHD. Some people don't like to be on this medication, and some do.

The Mystery of Ritchie Valens

ANDREA REYES * *age 14*
James Lick Middle School

Did you know that "Ritchie Valens" is not his real name?
His real name is Ricardo Esteban Valenzuela Reyes. He
had to change his name because Bob Keane, the president of
Del-Fi Records, said that there were too many Ricardos at that
time, and he choose Valens for Valenzuela to "broaden his
appeal."

Ritchie Valens was a Mexican-American singer. He was
born on May 13, 1941 in the San Fernando Valley region of Los
Angeles. His parents' names were Joseph Steven Valenzuela
and Concepción Reyes. Ritchie studied at Pacoima Junior High
School. In 1958, Ritchie quit school to concentrate on his career.

Ritchie was interested in making music on his own since
he was five years old. At Pacoima Junior High School, he used
to play the guitar and taught himself the drums. He joined a
band called "The Silhouettes" as a guitarist. Once the lead of
the band left, Ritchie left too because he wanted to try a solo
career. After that, Keane went to Pacoima Junior High School
and saw Ritchie's talent. Keane invited Ritchie to audition.

Keane liked Ritchie's talent, so Ritchie signed a contract with him. And that's how Ritchie changed his name.

In addition to changing Ritchie's name, Keane also recorded him playing guitar and singing for the first time. Keane did this because he wanted to see if Ritchie was actually ready for the next step. Some time later, Keane decided that Ritchie was ready to enter a band. The musicians in the band were Rene Hall and Earl Palmer. The first song Ritchie recorded at Golden Star was "Come On, Let's Go." After he recorded "Come On, Let's Go," he recorded "La Bamba" and "Oh, Donna." Those two songs were his biggest hits. The songs were in the movie *La Bamba* about Ritchie's life.

Before he died, Ritchie recorded a few songs. He went on a tour with Buddy Holly and JD "The Big Bopper" Richardson. On February 3, 1959, he died in a plane crash with Buddy Holly and "The Big Bopper." Since they died, people called that day the day the music died. Ritchie Valens was the youngest in the plane crash. He was barely eighteen years old.

Ritchie Valens is important because "La Bamba" was a Mexican song, but he made it into a rock'n'roll song. Alejandro Wolbert Perez is a PhD candidate from the University of California, Berkeley, and he said, "I think Valens had considerable impact on popular music overall, and Chicano Rock/Mexican-American popular music specifically, for a number of reasons."

Ritchie Valens is important to me because he made his own songs and did anything to show his talent. I've known of him since I was little, when I first saw his movie. I liked his story and researched more about him. I think people should care more about Ritchie Valens because he is awesome! And he hoped to be someone in life and to help his family to have a better life.

Obesity and Food

ABRAHAM VALLIN * *age 13*
James Lick Middle School

Obesity in the United States is one of the biggest problems
we have right now, next to sickness and the economy. Fast
food is trying to take the place of cigarettes. Everybody has
eaten fast food once. One fact that we know is that already in
the United States, one third of the population is overweight.
Another shocking fact is that half of the people born after the
millennium will get diabetes in their lifetime. All these facts
are evidence that fast food is slowly taking over the world.

If you do a test and decide to go to a local lower-income
neighborhood and then drive around and count all the fast
food restaurants and then the grocery stores, which do you
think will win? That's right, fast food. One example you can
also use is if you watch TV, you will see that more than half
of the commercials are about fast food. Don't think that the
United States government hasn't noticed all this; they are
trying to stop child obesity. Proof of this is Michelle Obama's
program, "Get Up and Play!" But a cheesy title isn't going to
stop all this, people. The government and big corporations are
going to have to have a hand in it. In one of your close lower-
income neighborhoods, there may be forty liquor stores and
one culturally inappropriate grocery store.

Food is something that your body needs. It's a necessity. If you eat too little, you're still hungry; if you eat too much, you're going to get cramps. Your body can only digest a certain amount of food at a time. People who eat food as an addiction, not as a necessity, eat it to relieve pain, stress, or even for recovery. Everybody has these kinds of triggers, whether it's losing your job or a family death. I think I've explained my point of view so far.

I interviewed the Executive Director from People's Grocery, which is an organization working to "build a local food system that improves the health and economy of West Oakland." The director's name is Nikki Henderson, and she is great. I asked her a couple questions about my subject involving obesity in the United States. I asked her, "Why do you think healthy food costs more than fast food?" Henderson said, "Unhealthy food tends to be much cheaper than healthy food. And the reason for that is because the government gives huge amounts of money to fast food companies." Obesity is a huge problem, and for us to stop fast food companies from earning more money, the government has to spend money on healthy food.

Ms. Henderson also responded by saying, "Bigger companies that are behind fast food, and that provide the convenience store food and liquor store food, they give them a lot of money to do it that way; that's called a subsidy." I think that James Lick Middle School students go to the corner store or Walgreens to buy junk food and soda, and it's not rare. People in the school usually see this on a daily basis. As time passes, more students will go there and start to get addicted. If you look at the evolution of "addiction," as I like to call it, first there was drinking, then smoking, now drugs, and now, and in our future, there will be a "food addiction." We all—and not just us, but also the government—need to contribute money to healthy food, like that you can get at Trader Joe's, Whole Foods, and other healthy places.

Take a microscope. Then take another microscope and look through that microscope into
the other microscope. Then take a magnifying
glass and look through all that. What do you
see? Nothing, that's what. That is a terrible set
up for an experiment. Put all that stuff away
and peruse the following pieces written by the
young authors from Nicole Moore and Virginia
Reyes's workshop "There's Poetry in an Atom."
Finding the not-so-tenuous connection between
art and science, these writers explore the world,
from the massive to the infinitesimally small. ✳

The Order of
the Narwhals

Finding Poetry in an Atom

Untitled

TAYLOR LEUNG * *age 14*
San Francisco School of the Arts

I

One day I went down to the beach
To ask the sea a few
Brief questions of his scope and size
To add to what I knew.
He waved with several foamy hands
And paused to clear his throat,
But I did find the breeze too harsh,
So I took to a boat.
He boomed with resonating voice,
"Have you not seen and heard
Of all the things I give and take
Without saying a word?
Too long have I been silent, and
I have the night to boast;
For years and centuries on end
I've ruled the sky and coast.
My seven daughters on this globe,
My clouds that cloak the sky,
All bring to you the rain you need
Without having to try.
Although I'm drained a thousand times,
My mouth is bottomless.
I'm fed by rivers bringing down
From mountains my essence.

One time (it was so long ago),
I covered e'en the land,
And though he said I may not do
So now I understand.
I feel the warmth, so close to Earth,
And hear the eyeless lives
Whisper the voiceless secrets of
Where Man has not set eyes,
What may say you, child of standing Earth,
This is the way I'll be,
Strong, though not the strongest one:
The storm, the life, the sea."

II

Once I looked through a microscope
To ask a cell a few
Brief questions of its scope and size
To add to what I knew.
It begged my pardon, telling me
It would have to be late.
So I looked on, while into two
It then did separate.
Its voice, though quiet, was resolute,
"I am not seen nor heard,
Yet I have served you long and hard
Without saying a word.
For long I've been invisible,
And though I'm not the most
 Long-lived or massive being alive
 I have the right to boast.
I'm infinitely smaller than the smallest bug alive
But look beyond my membrane-skin,
And see how I can thrive.
I'm like a little kingdom
With a nucleus as a king,
Directing other parts of me

And many other things.
Your town's huge generators make
Your electricity,
Though I have mitochondria
To make my energy.
And never am I by myself
I stand with billions more.
We build, we heal, we feel, we die,
And count ourselves not poor.
You need us, we are part of you,
And we need you as well.
For we uphold all forms of life.
Unseen, we are the Cell.

Tree Gossip

ELEANOR CHEN ✳ *age 13*
Alameda Country School

Beneath me, a boy plucks my leaves from the forest floor, placing them carefully into a near-overflowing box. California, the label reads.

My red-gold branches rustle in annoyance. California! Home of the most lazy and arrogant trees. No wonder the boy is mailing some of my beautiful, fallen garments. While my comrades and I shiver as the wind shakes through our limbs, the California trees are snug and comfortable in a scarf of green and red. I long for that warmth, but there are others that laugh. "We are not so arrogant," they say, shaking a blanket of snow from their branches. "We are proud to suffer through the world's cold."

I'm a California tree, but so what if I'm looked down upon? Gossip from other trees in Oregon or Washington scatters like their fallen autumn leaves, for in some places autumn is more than a few withering leaves and a spontaneous fleet of rainstorms. Distant from most cities in California, autumn is a great gale of red and orange, and a biting cold—rain dropping from the sky as though God were overwatering his flowerbed. Then there is winter: a few months filled with bitter clouds and snow. Other trees, naked and humbled from their fallen leaves, laugh at me. "Californians are dimwits," they laugh. "Stupid and too slow to relinquish their leaves and prepare for winter." But they're just jealous. So what if my jade jacket grows back sooner than theirs, embroidered with flowers and fruit? So what if I feel little cold—little reason to grow orange and red with shame. That's not my fault, is it?

The War of the Grapes

ZACH SOVEREIGN ✳ *age 12*
James Lick Middle School

At midnight I heard their call of war and the pounding at my
    door.
I knew what had happened—it was bound to come around,
the attack of the grapes
as they splattered in my face.
They put on their helmets,
climbed into the catapult,
then juice splattered across a pear
and suddenly I knew what to do
to save the world.
I opened my mouth and caught them there.
My cheeks bulged in their strappings. My teeth like a
    nutcracker,
I slew all those grapes,
but forever after, something
in my stomach was the matter.

Werewolves Let You Down

ELLA BOYD-WONG ✶ *age 12*
Creative Arts Charter School

Vampires are snobs. I do not have anything else to say on the matter, so I am going to move on to werewolves. Werewolves are amazing. Werewolves eat zombies and mutant mermaids. Werewolves eat everything. Yet, unlike mutant mummies, who usually eat bad things, werewolves are just like goats; they'll eat anything that is alive—except for plants.

Okay, okay, okay. Stop giving me that look. I know werewolves don't eat everything. But a lot of things! Come on, give me a break. Werewolves have a tendency to attack naked people more than regular people who are smart enough not to go nude in public. I guess it's the exposure to so much meat, too. And you know why I had to type all of this so slow? A werewolf ate my arm. The left one.

Now, I'm not talking about werewolves. I'm talking about *werewolves.* Not the puny, pathetic kind that Stephanie Meyer put in *Twilight*—I mean the kind that are gigantic, huge, big, ginormous, and all other synonyms for big. I mean the kind that have spiky fur, huge claws, enormous teeth, long tails, and huge muscles. They're bigger than bears and smaller than African elephants or houses.

Werewolves are usually described as having been discovered by Professor Edita Wallace, Professor Tortal Ben, and author Daniel Syrgur. Daniel Syrgur is dead now. He was attacked by five werewolf cubs when he described them as "small beings." They ate him.

There's this not-very-well-known theory: that freckles are more than just skin discolorations. Indeed, it's been proposed that, if you connect the dots, they spell out messages. The fact that we believe in this theory hasn't made us very popular at parties, but we're okay with that. We don't seem to be the only ones who believe in the power of our skin to communicate with the world. Eighth-grade English language learners in Mrs. Davis-Aceves's classroom at Everett Middle School have written bilingual poetry about the stories told by their skin. Think of it as an English/Spanish/Epidermis Rosetta Stone. *

The Richness of Our Skin

Eighth-Grade English-Language Learners Discover the Color of Poetry

The Feeling of My Skin

ELIA ABREGO ✳ *age 14*
Everett Middle School

My skin at dawn is like
A child who wakes up
Screaming and crying
When he doesn't feel
The warmth of his
Marvelous mother.

My skin is soft like
Rose petals, like the velvety
Pistil of a flower.

My skin is wheat-colored
Like a cup of hot chocolate
That makes me feel at peace
On April afternoons.

My skin is fresh as
A baby's, smooth and new.
My hand glides over the softness.

My skin dances like a spinning top
When I hear my mother say,
"Beloved daughter, your skin is
Tranquil, like mine."

My skin is like the
Shining sun that
Lights the darkness of
Nights.

My skin is like a leopard

Full of spots, like the universe
Full of stars.

The color of my skin radiates
Brightly like the sun on the
Beach, like gold in a mine.

My skin in the moonlight
Is as bright as looking
Into a mirror.

My skin is like an erupting
Volcano: when I'm mad
I become red.

Mi Skin Is Mi Ser

FERNANDA MARTINEZ ✳ *age 14*
Everett Middle School

My dark skin reminds me of my Mexican land.
My skin shines like the stars
That decorate my head below the ceiba tree.
My brown skin is my Mexican pride for
The fruit like the pineapple
With spikes and the peeling plantain.

My skin is the picture that I pull out
Of the river every time that it reflects who I am
And my color, to know who I am.

My chocolate skin is my mother
Who works every day for her children.

My skin rests like a fallen tree in a canyon
In the Valley of the Saints
Like when I sleep on my ranch.

My brown skin is like the candies of my lips
That I eat all the time, like the
Chocolates my grandma prepares to sell.

My muddy skin is like my family
Tired after playing in the countryside, like the
Birthmarks on my skin.
My skin is the light that guides me toward my future
And it makes me feel at home in the world.

My puma skin is the capotecas dancing in Oaxaca
Like the countrymen who stand by my side
When I need them.

My dark skin is like the Virgin of Tepeyac
Who stands in her basilica.
My pure skin is like Christ who's in heaven
Like the love that the holy spirit has given to me.

My skin is my Mexican land and the capotecas,
It represents my religion, my culture,
And my tradition like the
Red, white, and green of my flag as it descends.

The Beauty of My Skin

SUSANA ROBLES-DESGARDEN ✳ *age 12*
Everett Middle School

The beauty of my skin is the
mixture of my culture and my parents.
My skin is not light, much darker,
like the reflection of the sand
in the water.
My skin is French and Mexican
two cultures, different in many
ways. Both have pride in their hearts.

My skin feels all of my changes—my
emotion, my fears, and my joy—
celebrating my love for life.

If you touch my skin, it feels rough
like the bread served warm on
the Day of the Dead, November 2.

When the cool morning wind
blows each day from the pink
horizon, my skin listens like a snake
in the desert.

Robles is my last name and describes
me perfectly because my skin is
brown and strong like the oak tree.

My skin has eighty-eight spots like a free
leopard that runs in the field
and the scars that grow with each
year and the experience I've had in
my short life.

The beauty of my skin is Latina since
the first day I came to this earth, my
skin grows older with me and
will be with me for the rest of my life.

When I am angry my skin is red like
the sun that hides behind the waves
and the beaches of California.

The beauty of my skin is not just
on the outside, the beauty of my
skin is in my heart.

A Poem About My Skin

BRENDA MELARA ∗ *age 13*
Everett Middle School

My skin is as fine as sifted sand, and when you see and
touch it, you want to love it.

My skin is tasty, like Salvadorean pupusas, you want to eat
them as soon as you smell and see them.

My skin is Latina, my skin is wheat-colored, my skin is radiant like a Salvadorean.

Skin? There are so many kinds! But no one has skin like me
and my Latin people.

When I was born, my skin was as soft as a bird's wing but
now it is like a rose petal.

My skin thinks of you, cries for you, like the dewdrops that
run down my skin.

My skin laughs when you are near and cries when you are
far from me.

My skin is grateful like this: Thank you for life, thank you
for existence, thank you for making me happy, and thank
you for loving me.

My skin recognizes your good qualities when you are near
  me.

My skin needs you to forgive me for loving you so much.

You ever get that feeling that no one in the news is asking the questions that you want asked? What's the sound of one hand clapping? What came first: the chicken or the egg? Why did the chicken cross the road? How many chickens does it take to screw in a lightbulb? We get that feeling all the time; so we can see why the Everett community turns to the *Straight-Up News*. For the last seven years, the student journalists in Everett Middle School's Writers' Room have been finding the answers to the questions plaguing their peers. With bilingual articles ranging from exposés on cafeteria food to creative writing pieces imagining life in the Colonies, the *Straight-Up News* may not answer the chicken-related questions we have, but they were weird questions anyway. ✶

Straight–Up News

A Bilingual Newspaper from Everett Middle School

To Shakespeare or Not to Shakespeare

OLIVIA SCOTT * *age 13*
Everett Middle School

Friends, students, countrymen, lend me your ears. Shakespeare has been a popular writer for hundreds of years and now, after all this time, he can spread his writing to another school: Everett.

Shakespeare's birthday is unknown, but it is assumed to be April 23, 1564; he died fifty-two years later on the same day. He lived in Stratford-Upon-Avon, wrote approximately forty plays and 134 sonnets, and wrote all his plays for the acting group he was in. They were so good he even played for the queen, Queen Elizabeth I.

Shakespeare has been in your place many times before. It is supposed that Shakespeare enjoyed education at King's New School. The conditions were hard, as they sat on wooden benches from 6a.m. to 5 or 6p.m. with only two short breaks. He shows this in *As You Like It*, with a boy "creeping like a snail unwillingly to school." He also made up many commonly used words like bedroom, dawn, majestic, torture, and tranquil, as well as having many influences on people and books alike. Did you know people have counted how many commas he wrote? It totaled to 138,198. He also had many influences on novelists such as Herman Melville and Charles Dickens.

If it meant so much for these famous authors, wouldn't it be a good tool for middle-school students? Mrs. McNally-Norman, teacher at Blackheath High School, thinks "children should start learning Shakespeare at an earlier age so as to get used to his language and so they do not despair when they are suddenly faced with a seemingly incomprehensible soup of Shakespearean English." As Mrs. McNally-Norman said, if children were taught Shakespeare earlier, their minds would adapt to the older language and comprehend more of his "soup," so they would enjoy the story rather than be too stressed to enjoy his writing. Katerina Edgar, a student at Blackheath High School, says, "I like how he uses metaphors, similes, and word order to give a piece of writing its richness. I also like the way he uses rhythm to give his verse another dimension."

Even if you taught Shakespeare in a modern context it would benefit the students, as they can emphasize and relate to the scenes in Shakespeare's plays. Not only that, but it can benefit their writing as well as their use of the English language. Just as Isabella Scott said, "Shakespeare has made me the person I am today."

Skating in the Schoolyard

EBN DALY ✳ *age 13*
Everett Middle School

Skating in the schoolyard has been banned for a long time at Everett, but it is time for a change because many people would like to skate, including Alexia Castaneda and Egypt Hopkins. They both think it is a good sport, though it could be dangerous. Despite the ban, kids try to skate in the schoolyard, but their boards get taken away. The yard is big enough for four basketball courts, so the skaters could easily use a small area without interfering with other activities.

I think the school does not allow skating because of the risk of someone getting hurt. My mom says it's dangerous and a legal liability for the school, and she says that's why they banned it. I think she's right. The same goes for many other activities in the United States where government agencies or big corporations fear they will be sued if something goes wrong.

What this means is that many people, both children and adults, are prevented from doing things just because of remote risks. If prohibitions like this continue to proliferate, more and more Americans will become wimpy. Lots of adults disapprove of skateboarding because they think it may hurt people or public property, but that's all the more reason to set aside specific places for skating. As for the risk of injury, wearing a helmet is a good way to avoid serious problems.

What adults don't appreciate about skating is the sheer pleasure of it, the adrenaline rush it provides over and over again. When you almost fall and then save yourself, it's a real high. So is dropping off a raised surface into thin air or rolling fast down a half-pipe. These moves are so exciting that kids do them as often as they can. I go skating every day after school and also on the weekends. If skating was a part of the school experience, kids might like going to Everett, and the exercise would be good for them. Maybe all three grades should petition Mr. Curci to change the rules.

My proposal is that Everett should develop a set of rules for skating in the playground that would balance the school administrators' safety concerns with the skaters'. Here are a few examples:

· *Assign a security person to the skating area.*

· *Make all skaters wear a helmet.*

· *Cone off the area to stop skaters from running into other people.*

· *Set a limit to the number of people skating at any one time.*

With rules like these, I'm sure that a good balance could be achieved between the students' interests and the school administration.

Oil Spill Threatens Animals

ROSALIND BARRIOS * *age 12*
Everett Middle School

The 2010 oil spill endangered a lot of animals in the Gulf Coast of Mississippi. The oil spill affected animals by getting in their skin and eyes. Sharks, brown pelicans, birds, crabs, bluefin tuna, and many other animals were in danger. When the oil spill happened a lot of animals were laying eggs, and dolphins were having babies. Lots of animals and their eggs were in trouble because of the oil spill.

The scientists helped sea turtles. Many of the turtles were found oiled. They were cleaned and nursed back to health. Each turtle was tagged with satellite tracker. They cleaned them so well that they felt healthy. Turtles were being released into unfamiliar waters, and each turtle found their way back to their natural habitat.

The causes for the animals' death were that the water was cold and that there was oil. One of the things that happened was that the animals were not used to being in a new environment. Scientists moved a large number in the Gulf of Mexico out of their place. A lot of animals died and it was sad for the scientists.

A lot of animals died in the oil spills. They reported that three hundred turtles died in the Mississippi. Two endangered manatees died near the Gulf Coast. The manatees died because they were in the cold water but they belonged in warmer water. A lot of animals died because they did not know where they were. They were confused.

Video Games

MARCEL BROWN ✳ *age 13*
Everett Middle School

To move, or not to move? Video gaming is evolving, and players have to get up and take action. The newest thing in the video game world is motion gaming. Some of the options are the Wii, Playstation Move, and Kinect for Xbox 360.

The good thing about motion gaming is that motion gaming is more fun because you are interactive with the game, instead of just sitting down on the couch and pressing buttons. With the Wii, there are a lot of different games because the Wii was out first. But the Playstation Move has the best graphics. It's like watching HDTV. You can see the sweat dripping down their faces. The Xbox 360 has no controller, so you interact most with the game you are playing.

One of the bad things about motion gaming with a controller is that you are at the risk of breaking stuff, like your dad's TV. The Wii and the Playstation Move both require a controller.

Even though all of the systems have their own individual good and bad things about them, I like the Kinect the best. First of all, there is no controller. This is my favorite feature. Second of all, there are no straps or wires that you have to attach to yourself. Last but not least, the games are very exhilarating and exciting.

Horror Movies!
Scream 3

CORDELL C. LYNCH, JR. * *age 13*
Everett Middle School

There are many people who play the role of the masked killer in the *Scream* movies. Unlike other horror films, the killer always gets killed. *Scream 3* is about a girl named Sydney who has a terrible past, and a director is making a movie called *Stab*, based on her life. Sydney is worried about what will happen. In *Scream 3,* this killer is killing the cast of *Stab* in the order of the movie script.

But what I don't get is why the main character never dies. Here is how the people in the movies could have survived: Take all of the phone cords out of the wall and don't leave the doors unlocked. Also never, ever have anything on the stove or in the microwave. And never have any company coming over, because that is the main thing that happens when characters get killed. And that is how I think people could survive the movie.

Scream 3 is my favorite movie. One of the reasons why I like this movie is the way the timing is set up when the killer is going to kill someone. He calls and makes his victim very scared. Another reason is when the killer gets ready to kill, he lets each character know he is coming and gets to the point. One of the funny scenes in the movie that I like is when the cast of *Stab* meets the people they are portraying. The actress playing Gale Weathers says to the real Gale Weathers, "If someone wants to kill me, I'll be with you, and since he really wants to kill you, he won't kill me, he'll kill you. Make sense?" This movie combines horror and comedy.

Letters from the Colonies

ISAILEVI LOPEZ ✳ *age 14*
Everett Middle School

SEPTEMBER 37

Dear DeMozart,

It is week three since I've arrived in the colony of Connecticut. Feels like I've been here for only three days. Well, I must insist that I tell you about my journey and arrival. The seas were rough. It was long and exhausting, storms at night and calm waters in the morning. Felt like I was in the seas for years and weeks. Then finally I arrived. I was welcomed by the founder of the colony of Connecticut—Thomas Hooker, he's a puritan like you and me, Moz. He told me he started a colony because of the Anglican Church. He said, "They were too fancy, and I want church services to be simpler." Hooker believes that the government should be based on the free consent of the people to whom belong the choice of public magistrates. He is trying to get a charter for the colony of Connecticut.

Well now, let me tell you about my daily life. Recently, about two weeks ago, I found a job as a ship builder where we have to build ships for whaling. We're using oak trees.

The job is a lot different from my job back home of milking cows and raising cattle. Every morning I wake up, eat cornbread and trout, then head off to work. There, like I said, I am working on a very beautiful ship. Then, when I'm done working, I eat a bit of salmon with tomato and go to sleep. I do this Monday through Friday. On Saturdays I go hunting deer with my friends. We've killed quite a few deer. After hunting, I head off to help Mr. Thoven de Lion. He's one of very few teachers here in Connecticut. He's teaching many children, and that why I help him with his students. I'm also teaching the children psalms. Next, after this, I head off to go eat a bit of corn and carrots and go to bed after. Then it's Sunday, time for church. Services are only one hour long and we don't have to return! Oh, and did you know there is a colony named New Haven nearby? It is very strict there. I am glad that I settled here. They don't even have a charter in that colony. I am glad that I left Massachusetts too. Life's better here, in my opinion. The punishments are the same: you are put to death if you murder, commit treason, or commit piracy. Other crimes are punished lesser, like robbery. Did I tell you about the class differences? Well, if not, let me. Here slaves are the lowest class of them all. Next are the farmhands, and the middle class is made up of farmers and artisans. That's about it. Well, I've got to go, goodbye!

Sincerely, your apprentice,
Isailevi Lopez

Sometimes the thing you're looking for is right in front of your face, you just don't know how to see it. Like if an elephant was really close to you, you might not know what it was. But if you looked closer, you could see that it had hairs and little bugs. If you looked even closer, you could see little bugs on the bugs, and bugs on those bugs, and they're all really gross and you're like, I'm gonna throw up and then—Sorry. What does that have to do with anything? Here are some wonderful pieces from *Look Closer*, our bilingual publication from After-School Tutoring students, coordinated and edited by our Programs Director, Vickie Vertiz. Get it really close up to your face. You'll see things you never knew were there. ✳

Look Closer

Stories, Poems, and a Play from 826 Valencia's After-School Tutoring

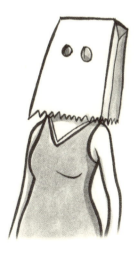

The Carrot and the Horse, Part 2

JASMINE CHOCHOM ∗ *age 8*
Edison Charter Academy

Once upon a time, there was a carrot who loved another carrot. The horse said to one of the carrots, "Would you be with me?" and she said, "Sorry, but I have someone."

Max the horse was sad, so he left. The other carrot said, "Who is your boyfriend?" She said, "You are my boyfriend." He said, "Oh." So they lived happily ever after.

My World

KENNY DZIB ✳ *age 11*
Edison Charter Academy

In my world I see many trees.
In my world there is never any war.
In my world there are no such things as money, poor, or rich.
In my world everyone is united.
In my world there is always someone to ask for help.
In my world everyone listens.
In my world there is no leader, everyone is treated equally.
In my world you could travel wherever without permission
    because land is free.
In my world there are no enemies, just family.
In my world all are permitted at school.
In my world we respect nature not abuse it.
In my world there is always hope.

My Pet Has One Hundred Legs

MELODY RUELAS ✳ *age 8*
Edison Chater Academy

My pet has one hundred legs. He has one hundred mouths on his legs. He eats one hundred things at a time, like cupcakes, fingers, brains, and soda, but he is a nice pet. He likes the colors green and purple, like me. I love him and he loves me. The end.

A Penny

ALEJANDRA MEDINA ✳ *age 10*
St. James School

Once upon a time, there was a penny. He lived on a farm. He was very new. There was this cow that collected pennies, and he always got ugly old pennies.

So one day his owner was milking him and the cow saw a shiny light. It was coming from the penny, and he got so excited that he kicked his owner and ran to the penny. The penny got scared and squeaked. Then the cow took him, and then later on he was in the cow's room. Soon enough the penny ran out and kept running and running until it got lost and met a lot of quarters, nickels, and dimes. The quarters were show-offs, the nickels always gave high-fives, and the dimes had ten doughuts, and there was only one penny, but soon they became friends and the penny never went back to the cow. The cow was sad because he went back into his room and the penny was gone. The cow started crying and crying and crying.

The best friends were always hanging out. They went to the movies and then they got a pizza and only ate the crumbs because they got full after like five of them.

A Little Bird

KAROLINA OCHOA ✳ *age 7*
Edison Charter Academy

There was once a little bird who went to school and he was very shy. On the first day of school he was scared. He took the bus to go to school. He became friends with a lot of people. Soon he went back home. When it was dinnertime he was talking about how his day went at school. So he went every day.

One day he was sick so he couldn't go for three whole days. He was getting bored. He wanted to play with his friends. He had to eat in bed. He ate soup and a big salad. He went to the doctor, who said he had to stay in bed for another three days. The bird was very sad. He wanted to go to school. Then one day he got better, went to the bus stop, and waited for the bus. When he walked onto the bus, the lights were off and everyone was happy. Everyone had a gift for him.

I Love the Rain

GIUSEPPE PACHECO ✳ *age 9*
Edison Charter Academy

I love the rain becaues it is fun when you play outside. Last time I was in the rain with my friend Yovana, she asked me if I wanted to use her umbrella and I did not want to. Instead I got wet. Then I came to 826 Valencia and everybody thought I was sweating, but I was wet.

The Beastly Curse

CITLALLI AGUILAR * *age 10*
Alvarado Elementary School

When Ms. Wolverine was little, her mom wanted to be the prettiest woman in the world and so gave her daughter cursed money, making her ugly and ensuring that Ms. Wolverine would never rival her in beauty. Since then, Ms. Wolverine has been cursed with ugliness.

SCENE

> **MS. WOLVERINE** *grabs her makeup and puts it on her beastly face. It takes her about an hour to put on her makeup. She uses all her makeup, and it all ends up on her face.*

MS. WOLVERINE: *(Stares at her reflection)* AAAAAHHHH-HHHHHHHHHHHHH!!!!! *(Facing the audience)* I don't know why Wolverine is with me if he doesn't like me at all. We would make the best, cutest, and richest couple if I were beautiful. I will go to that creepy witch-doctor guy. For sure he'll turn me into a beautiful girl!

Meanwhile, **WOLVERINE** *and* **SUPER GIRL** *are hanging out in the living room.*

WOLVERINE: Really? You think I like her? Ha! You are so weird! I really think that she is the daughter of the ugly bear in the most wild forest

SUPER GIRL: Then why do you go out with her? This is really the funniest moment of my life. This moment is so funny and ridiculous it could go on YouTube.

WOLVERINE: I really don't understand. She has so much money. I really love that money! It can rain with money in the mansion.

MS. WOLVERINE is listening to the conversation and she feels really ugly. Nothing could make her feel even uglier.

MS. WOLVERINE: (*Walking into the living room*) What?! You really only like my money?

WOLVERINE: No, it's not true! Whatever you think, it's not true. AT ALL.

MS. WOLVERINE: Oh yeah? I always felt like I could never suffer when you hug me, but now I feel like you don't love me at all.

WOLVERINE: Forget about everything I said! I LOVE YOU!!!!!

MS. WOLVERINE: No, you do not!

SUPER GIRL: Wolverine, that is not what you said. Nothing in there is right at all. You said you are only with her because she is rich and that it rains buckets of money in the mansion.

MS. WOLVERINE: See, that is what I'm talking about. You don't love me at all, and we can't get married because you don't love me. What name can I name you? "The Big Furry Wolf Who Only Loves Money and Cheats on Me." Who is your real girlfriend? Ms. BettyBop?

SUPER GIRL: Hey, look on the bright side—

WOLVERINE: (*Interrupting*) There is no bright side, you understudy of Superman!

MS. WOLVERINE: Yeah, you're right Super Girl. Wolverine, you don't love me at all. Maybe it's only the money you want. Is that beautiful to you?

SUPER GIRL: (*to* **MS. WOLVERINE**) Hey squirrelfriend! You're talking hard now! (*to* **WOLVERINE**) You just got topped! Wolverine?

WOLVERINE: Grrrrrrrrrrrrrrrrr...

SUPER GIRL: (*Mocking*) OH! Look at that baby growling! Uh-oh!

MS. WOLVERINE: STOP! STOP!

WOLVERINE: (*Getting angry at* **SUPER GIRL** *for making fun of him*) GRRRRRRRRRRRR!!!!

MS. WOLVERINE: I love you a lot, but I don't want to be rich any more. Because then I know you will be cheating on me with BettyBop.

SUPER GIRL: Uh-huh uh-huh uh-huh. You made every sentence in there right, squirrelfriend! Oh! Here comes a tiger. (*Moves her hand like a tiger*) Rawr!

MS. WOLVERINE: Here you go! Take my money! I don't want it anymore!

Free of the curse, **MS. WOLVERINE** *becomes the prettiest woman in the world. (SOUND CUE) She lets down her hair*

SUPER GIRL: OOOOOOOOH! (*She faints because* **MS. WOLVERINE** *is so beautiful*)

WOLVERINE: OMG! You should be a model!

MS. WOLVERINE: TMI. I was born for that!

WOLVERINE: Grrrrrrrrrrrrrrr. Grrrrrrr.

WOLVERINE *falls in love with* **MS. WOLVERINE**. *He gets down on one knee to propose.*

WOLVERINE: Would you marry me?

MS. WOLVERINE: Oh, no way. You want to cheat on me again, you big furry loser? How about you go cry to BettyBop about how you want me back? I am so cool because I make your favorite snacks, I sing, and I am very beautiful. What did you ever do for me? Huh? What have you done for BettyBop? (*In a funny voice*) Or "BoppyBop"? She told me you went to the beach with her and told her you didn't love me at all. Then you invited her to a restaurant and paid for her dish! I always had to pay for my dish and your dish! Oh yeah, and I'm talented! I don't need you.

WOLVERINE: But I've been with you for more than ten years!

MS. WOLVERINE: I love my life now that I am away from the curse! And you should start looking for beautiful, talented people like me. Treat them very nicely. Pay for their food— not like you did for me. Be kind to them. You can stay with me until you find the next girl of your dreams.

*SUPER GIRL wakes up. She and **MS. WOLVERINE** put their arms around each other's shoulders and walk off happily.*

THE END

Have you ever played that game where you try to guess how many jellybeans are in a jar and whoever's closest wins a prize? Well, in this next section there's going to be a lot of information about all the things we do at 826 Valencia. Things like book projects, and after-school tutoring, and all sorts of other whatnot. The other thing you'll see is who we are, and most of the people we are are volunteers. The list is pretty long. This is where the jellybean counting thing comes in. If you can guess, just by looking, how many volunteers we have, we'll give you a really great prize. Whoever gets within twenty-five first, without going over, wins. Email guesses to justin@826valencia.org *

About 826
Valencia

The People of 826 Valencia

THE STAFF OF 826 VALENCIA
Anne Farrah *Development Director*
Emilie Coulson *Programs Director*
Jorge Garcia *Programs Director*
Justin Carder *Pirate Store Manager & Publishing Director*
Lauren Hall *Programs Coordinator*
Leigh Lehman *Executive Director*
María Inés Montes *Design Director*
Miranda Tsang *Programs Coordinator*
Raúl Alcantar *Programs Assistant*
Valrie Sanders *Finance & Operations Manager*
Yalie Kamara *Volunteer & Events Coordinator*

THE BELOVED INTERNS OF 826 VALENCIA
Winter/Spring 2011
Alex Lannon
Alicia Jacobs
Alyse Oneto
Amada Foushee
Amy Langer
Blythe Tai
Christian Rongavilla
Darshita Mistry
Devin Asaro

Erin Canoy
John Wilson
Julia Roma
Justine Macauley
Lauren Mulkey
Lisa Sig Olesen
Mariel Keener
McKenna Stayner
Zainab Rupawalla

Summer 2011
Andrea Torres
Erica McMath
Gina Cargas
Hannah Vick
Jenna Finkle
Joel Morley
Jordan Clare-Rothe
Josselyn Bonila

Katie King Rumford
Kristen Libero
Lizzy Martin
Martín Arellano
Moss Turpan
Naomi Stark
Osvaldo Marquez
Simone Loudd

THE 826 VALENCIA BOARD OF DIRECTORS

Abner Morales

Alexandra Quinn

Barb Bersche

Brian Gray

Mary Schaefer

Matt Middlebrook

Michael Beckwith

Olive Mitra

Thomas Mike

Vendela Vida

826 VALENCIA CO-FOUNDERS

Dave Eggers, Nínive Calegari

THE THOUSANDS OF VOLUNTEERS, TUTORS, & WORKSHOP TEACHERS AT 826 VALENCIA

Aaron Colton, Aaron Kayce, Aaron Kierbel, Aaron McManus, Aaron Sanchez, Aaron Shapiro, Aaron Spector, Aaron Staple, Aaron Wells, Abbey Levantini, Abby Orellana, Abby Ramsden, Abby Wittman, Abigail Jacobs, Abigail Wick, Abner Morales, Abrahim El Gamal, Adam J. Blane, Adam Chapman, Adam Chipkin, Adam Cimino, Adam Daum, Adam Donovan, Adam Estes, Adam Faber, Adam Gerston, Adam Healton, Adam Hurly, Adam Johnson, Adam Lane, Adam Lauridsen, Adam Metz, Adam Paganini, Adam Rugel, Adam Rzepka, Adam Shemper, Adam Willumsen, Adam Wilson, Adelaide Goldfrank, Adele Shea, Aden Clay, Adin Eichler, Adolpho Meija, Adria Hou, Adrian Agredo, Adrian Kudler, Adriana Pena, Adriana Stevens, Adrianna Ely, Adrianne Koteen, Adrienne Julia Mahar, Adrienne LaBonte, Adrienne So, Ai Nguyen, Aidan O'Flynn, Aileen Pagdanganan, Aimee Goggins, Aimee Haeussler, Aimee Male, Aimee O'Donnell, Aislinn Ryan, Aja Desmond, Alaine Bowling, Alaine Panitch, Alan Becker, Alan Masinter, Alan Mutter, Alan Schacter, Alan Simpson, Alana DeRiggi, Alana Garcia, Alana Roman, Alanda Levinson-LaBrosse, Alanna Hale, Alberto Reyes, Alec Binnie, Alethia Shih, Alex Abreu, Alex Altman, Alex Brasfield, Alex Carp, Alex Chisholm, Alex Collins, Alex Giardino, Alex Haber, Alex Hooker, Alex Hurst, Alex Ludlum, Alex Mayor, Alex Mensing, Alex Mlley, Alex Nichols, Elizabeth Weld Nolan, Alex Palhegyi, Alex Portilla, Alex Rosenthal, Alex Scott, Alex Tenorio, Alex Venegas, Alex Wellen, Alex Young, Alexa Hilal, Alexa Kelly, Alexander Bien, Alexander Carpenter, Alexander Marais, Alexander Nemick, Alexander Slotnick, Alexander Vogel, Alexandra Chang, Alexandra Creighton, Alexandra Crotta, Alexandra Cruse, Alexandra Dove, Alexandra Kostoulas, Alexandra Nell, Alexandra Palazzolo, Alexandra Post, Alexandra Roger, Alexandra Rutherfurd, Alexandra Sheehan, Alexandra Slessarev, Alexandra Washkin, Alexandros Acedo, Alexavier Robinson, Alexei Bien, Alexandra Quinn Spolyar Alexis Brayton, Alexis Fajardo, Alexis Filippini, Alexis Iammarino, Alexis Lynch, Alexis Ohanian, Alexis Perlmutter, Alexis Waggoner, Alexis Wright, Alfa Villaflor, Ali Lanzetta, Ali Nazar, Ali Neff, Ali Van Doren, Alia Moore, Alia Salim, Alia Thiel, Alice Husak, Alice Joy, Alice Petty, Alice Wu, Alicia Bleuer, Alicia McKean, Alinta Williams, Alisa Dodge, Alisa Ostarello, Alison Alkire, Alison Chase, Alison Constantine, Alison Datz, Alison Doernberg, Alison Ekizian, Alison Greenberg, Alison Meier, Alison Powell, Alison Sperling, Alison Thompson, Alison Wannamaker, Aliza Aufrichtig, Aljay "Jay" Pascua, Allan Dorr, Allie Holly-Gottlieb, Allison Athens, Allison Boyd,

Allison Campbell, Allison Cole, Allison Davis, Allison Domicone, Allison Foley, Allison Lee, Allison Logue, Allison Muir, Allison Slater, Allison Taylor, Allyson Quibell, Alma Schneider, Alpana Katre, Alpana Soni, Althea Acas, Althea James, Alvin Chan, Alvin Orloff, Alysa Jo Dils, Alysha Naples, Alyssa Fernandez-Isla, Alyssa Martin, Alyssa Perry, Alyssa Tsukako, Alyssa Ure, Amanda Anselmino, Amanda Coggin, Amanda Dennis, Amanda Dominguez, Amanda Fowler, Amanda Johnson, Amanda Machi, Amanda Margulies, Amanda Jones, Amanda McKerracher, Amanda Moore, Amanda Oschsner, Amanda Reed, Amanda Smart, Amanda Meth, Amanda Tanner, Amanda Wolff, Amani Hanafi, Amaya Rivera, Amber Lowi, Amber Matthews, Ambri Pukhraj, Amelia Ashton, Amelia Fay-Berquist, Amelia Mularz, Amelia Wen, Amelie Lipman, Amelie Wen, Amethyst Ware, Ami Cuneo, Ami Schiess, Amick Boone, Amie Marvel, Amie Nenninger, Amie Spitler, Amity Armstrong, Amity Bacon, Amol Ray, Amy Atkinson, Amy Berkowitz, Amy Boulanger, Amy Braun, Amy Burton, Amy Chan, Amy Choi, Amy Cohen, Amy Compeau, Amy Crossin, Amy Dietz, Amy Donsky, Amy Goldwitz, Amy Guittard, Amy Huber, Amy Keyishian, Amy Linder, Amy Lyman, Amy Magruder, Amy Meaux, Amy Miles, Amy Natsumi Horton, Amy O'Hair, Amy Pham, Amy Popovich, Amy Rees, Amy Roa, Amy Seaman, Amy Skryja, Amy Steinberg, Amy Whitesides, Amy Wilson, Amy Young, Amy Zimmerman, Ana Arayo, Ana Campoy, Ana Chavier, Ana Ghosh, Ana Homayoun, Ana Lantigua, Ana Moraga, Ana Saldamando, Ana Schwartzman, Ana Soriano, Ana Weibgen, Analisa Svehaug, Anami Sheppard, Anastasia Goodstein, Anastasia Pahules, Anastasia Richardson, Anderson Jonas, Andra Cernavskis, Andre Carter, Andre Vallin, Andrea Arata, Andrea Donohoe, Andrea Drugan, Andrea Fender, Andrea Gousen, Andrea Gutierrez, Andrea Lane, Andrea Laue, Andrea Lee Mitchell, Andrea Navin, Andrea Orr, Andrea Hall, Andrea Ortiz, Andrea Paniagua, Andrea Turner, Andrea Urmanita, Andreas Trolf, Andrew Alder, Andrew Barton, Andrew Chamings, Andrew Connors, Andrew Dudley, Andrew Hammond, Andrew Kitchell, Andrew Lee, Andrew Leland, Andrew Linderman, Andrew Lipnick, Andrew Mahlstedt, Andrew McLane, Andrew Miller, Andrew Price, Andrew Rittenberg, Andrew Rosenberg, Andrew Simmons, Andrew Strombeck, Andrew Sywak, Andrew Tan, Andrew Ulmer, Andrew Vennari, Andrew Strickman, Andrew Volkert, Andrew Wagner, Andrew Ziaja, Andrew Zingg, Andro Hsu, Andy Jones, Andy Le, Andy Proehl, Andy Raskin, Andy Wong, Aneela Ahmed, Aneeska Capur, Angela Hernandez, Angela Hokanson, Angela Holms, Angela Hur, Angela Ingel, Angela Kung, Angela Lucia, Angela Penny, Angela Roberts, Angela Tafoya, Angela Tsang, Angelica Nava, Angelica Perez, Angelina Lai, Angie Landau, Angie Needels, Angie Powers, Angie Yuan, Anisha Tekade, Angelique Lobo, Anisse-Marie Gross, Anita Schiller, Anita Shah, Anita Trachte, Anjel Van Slyke, Anjelais Diaz, Ann Wang, Ann Wemeier, Ann-Marie Askew, Ann Barnett, Ann Clegg, Ann Elliott, Anne Marie Hogan, Ann Krilanovich, Ann Maley, Ann Marie Cavosora, Ann Marie Harrison, Anna Armstrong, Anna Bullard, Anna Crawley, Anna Cvitkovic, Anna Gast, Anna Hirsch, Anna Hurley, Anna King, Anna Marie Lund, Anna O'Neil, Anna Pickard, Anna Tome, Anna Waldman-Brown, Anna Walters, Anne Cramer, Anne Diaz, Anne Dowie, Anne Hector, Anne Hedges, Anne Holder, Anne Yang Hwang, Anne Jaffe, Anne Kaplan, Anne Kenney, Anne Feld Lowell, Anne Posten, Anne Swan,

Anne Lockwood Thompson, Anne Wintroub, Anne Zimmerman, Anne-Marie Cordingly, Anne Marie Townsend, Annelies Zijderveld, Annie Baxter, Annie Carmichael, Annie Carter, Annie Chiles, Annie Countryman, Annie Ha, Annie Happel, Annie Hunt, Annie Johnson, Annie Lo, Annie Marie Moore, Annie Pennell, Annie Walsh Robinson, Annika "Nikki" Grattan, Antal Polony, Anthea Tjuanakis, Annie Tomlin, Anthony "Nino" Boles-King, Anthony Bushong, Anthony Carrillo, Anthony Firestine, Anthony Leonard, Anthony Macias, Anthony Sanchez, Antigone Slavko, Antionette Tran, Antonia Giannoccaro, Antonia Hitchens, Antonia Oakley, Antonio D'Souza, Anya Diamond, Apphia Williams, April Bennett, April Berg, April DeCosta, April Eberhardt, April Goldman, April Sinclair, Archana "Tess" Padma Burra, Arena Reed, Ari Messer, Ari Vais, Ariana Schoellhorn, Ariel Aver, Ariel Balter, Ariel Dovas, Ariel Fintushel, Ariel Morris, Ariel Quirolo, Ariel Rokem, Ariel Rosen, Arlo Crawford, Arne Johnson, Arnold Posada, Arree Chung, Ariel Sugar, Arthur Bollmann, Arthur Bueno, Arul Thangavel, Arya Kamangar, Arya Kamangar, Arya Rafie, Asbe Darcy, Ashia De la Bastide, Ashley Dumich, Ashley Finn-Lucio, Ashley Kalemijian, Ashley Kanigher, Ashley Marshall, Ashley Nelson, Ashley Perryman, Ashley Rouen, Ashley Wells, Ashley Weatherford, Ashli Lewis, Ashok Parameswaran, Ashwin Seshagiri, Astra Johnson, Atalanta Powell, Athena Mak, Atosa Babbaoff, Atul Varma, Audrey Bower, Audrey Cortes, Audrey Ferber, Audrey Glazier, Audrey Khuner, Audrey Kim, Audrey Moilanen, Audrey Molina, August Cole, August d'Alessan, August Kleinzahler, Austin Hoffmann, Austin Kim, Austin Quig-Hartman, Austin Stewart, Ava Mees List, Aviel Chang, Azmeer Salleh, Bailee DesRocher, Bailey Eells, Baldwin Tong, Barajas Leticia, Barclay F. Corbus, Barb Hoffer, Barbara Bersche, Barbara Bradbury, Barbara Konecky, Barbara Robinson, Barbara Szerlip, Barbara Yu, Barry Weeks, Barton Creeth, Bay Hudner, Becka Robbins, Becky Newman, Becky Wolf, Belinda Man, Ben Bayol, Ben Brewer, Ben Brosnahan, Ben Burke, Ben Campbell, Ben Castanon, Ben Fuchs, Ben Fullerton, Ben Johnson, Ben Ogden, Ben Paviour, Ben Polansky, Ben Russo, Ben Shear, Ben Stefonik, Ben Zotto, Ben Zulauf, Benberry Freeman, Benjamin Boudreaux, Benjamin Morgan, Benjamin Palmer, Benjamin Schlotz, Benjamin Slater, Benjamin Yang, Bennett Steinmuller, Bernadette Blanco, Beryl Rae Levy, Beth DeAraujo, Beth Gerber, Beth Lemke, Beth Levin, Beth Macom, Beth Sears, Beth Wilson, Bethany Currin, Bethany Polentz, Betial Asmerom, Betsy Barnes, Betsy Keever, Beverley Talbott, Bevin McBride, Bianca Chavez, Bianca Levan, Bianca Woods, Bill Harvey, Billy Terrell, Bita Nazarian, Bitner Jenny, BJune Speaker, Blaine Hunt, Blair Wellington, Blaise Simpson Dugan, Blake Love, Blake Robin, Blake Robin, Blake Shurtz, Blythe Duffield, Bob Stock, Bobby Cupp, Bonnie Baron, Bonnie Begusch, Bonnie Chan, Bonnie Ogg, Bonnie Tsui, Bonny Hinners, Bonny Hinners, Booh Edourado, Bozena Mercedes Morawski, Brad Leibin, Brad Phifer, Brad Stone, Brady Welch, Brandi Brooks, Brandi Stansbury, Brandon Bussolini, Brandon Kenneth Cole, Brandon Vaden, Brandt Wicke, Bree Humphries, Brenda Natoli, Brandon Smith, Brendan Ternus, Brenna Burns, Brent Fitzgerald, Brent Jordheim, Brian Anthony, Brian Allen, Brian Bernbaum, Brian Chen, Brian Dane, Brian Dutro, Brian Gray, Brian Haagsman, Brian Hansen, Brian Jameson, Brian Kolm, Brian Martin, Brian Mazo, Brian Moss, Brian Myrtetus, Brian Pfeffer, Brian "Doc Pop" Roberts, Brian Hale Park, Brian W.

Rogers, Brian Smith, Brian Stannard, Briana Bispo, Brianna Collins, Brianna
Evans, Brianna Jewell, Brianna Smith, Bridget Mackinson, Brie Mazurek, Brigid
O'Neil, Brigitte Tu, Brigitte Zimmerman, Brion Baer, Brita Thompson, Brittany
Alvy, Brittany Fiore-Silfaust, Brittany Horman, Bronwen Wyatt, Brooke Dabalos,
Brooke Wilock, Bruce Adams, Bruce Genaro, Bruce Mckay, Bruce Nye, Bryan
Anthony, Bryan Wiley, Brye Schoeder, Bryn Dyment, Bryn Laux, Brynn Gelbard,
Bud Teasley, Burt Meyer, Byron Perry, C.J. Martinez, Cabala Windle, Cady Sitkin,
Caedmon Haas, Cailie Skelton, Caitlin Abber, Caitlin Appert, Caitlin Chiller,
Caitlin Craven, Caitlin Crowe, Caitlin Dunn, Caitlin Jennings, Caitlin McGinn,
Caitlin McKewan, Caitlin Murphy, Caitlin Ross, Caitlin Ryan, Caitlin Sandberg,
Caitlin Van Dusen, Caitlin Wilson, Caitlyn Corson, Caleb Garling, Caleb
Goodman, Caleb Leisure, Caleb van den Cline, Calla Devlin, Cameron Burch,
Cameron Clark, Cameron Dunning, Cameron Tuttle, Camila Geld, Camilo
Alejandro Sanchez, Cammie Clark, Candace Bagley, Candace Chen, Candace
Jensen, Candice Benge, Candice Hansen, Candice Liu, Cara Jones, Carey
Fay-Horowitz, Cari Tuna, Carin Capolongo, Carina Ost, Carl Mickelson, Carl
Siegel, Carla Carpio, Carla Doughty, Carla Gassner, Carlos Alderete, Carlos
Ramirez, Carmel Hagen, Carmel Wroth, Carmela Cancelliere, Carol Arnold,
Carol Dorf, Carol Hazenfield, Carol Jun-Roberts, Carol McKee, Carol Morita,
Carol Richards, Carol Treadwell, Carol Weinstein, Carole Elizabeth Perry, Carole
Snitzer, Carolina Braunschweig, Caroline Bracco, Caroline Casper, Caroline
Ching, Caroline Hollnagel, Caroline Kraus, Caroline Kwok, Caroline Nguyen,
Caroline Valentine, Caroline Wong, Carolyn Alburger, Carolyn Dicinson, Carolyn
Falkenberg, Carolyn Gan, Carolyn Hart, Carolyn Ho, Carolyn Jones, Carolyn
Reid, Carolyn Schultz, Carolyn Wilson-Koerschen, Carrie Cunningham, Carrie
Donovan, Carrie Galbraith, Carrie LeCompte, Carrie Mitchell, Carrie Scheib,
Carrie Williams, Carrie "Charly" Godwin, Carson Beker, Carson Chodos, Carter
Quigg, Cary Hammer, Cary Tennis, Cary Troy, Casey Cushing, Casey Flax, Casey
Henry, Casey Scott, Casey Selover, Casey Young, Cassandra Giraldo, Cassidy
Smith, Cassiel Chadwick, Cat Aboudara, Cat Crawford, Cat Kim, Catalina Ruiz-
Healy, Catharine Wargo, Catherine Brady, Catherine Cole, Catherine Gacad,
Catherine Heckendorf, Catherine Hollis, Catherine Lanter, Catherine Miller,
Catherine Mongeon, Catherine Pantsios, Catherine Plato, Catherine Potter,
Catherine Silvestre, Catherine Tillery, Catherine Woods, Cathi Murphy, Cathy
Kornblith, Cathy Remick, Cathy Tran, Cecilia Boyed, Cecily Anders, Celeste
McMullin, Celeste Perron, Celeste Ramos, Celine Bezamat-Homer, Celine
Lombardi, Chad Lent, Chad Lott, Chad Slife, Chan Tai, Chana Morgenstern,
Chance Fraser, Channing Sargent, Chantal Forfota, Chantal O'Keeffe, Chapin
Boyer, Charissa Owens, Charlene St. John, Charles Boodman, Charles Brady,
Charles Carriere, Charles Dahan, Charles Day, Charles Lantz, Charles Osthimer,
Charles Presley III, Charles Schoonover, Charles Wincorn, Charles-Henri Gros,
Charlie Crespo, Charlie Johnson, Charlie Pizarro, Charlie Radin, Charlie Wylie,
Charlotte Carr, Charlotte Makoff, Charlotte Ng, Charlotte Petersen, Charlotte
Sheedy, Chaz Reetz-Laiolo, Chellis Ying, Chelsea Clark, Chelsea Kouns, Chelsea
Lin, Chelsea Martin, Chelsea Wong, Cheri Hickman, Cheri Lucas, Cheryl Alvarez,
Cheryl Hendrickson, Cheryl Holzmeyer, Cheryl Taruc, Chet Martine, Chid
Liberty, Chino Baluyut, Chloe Gates, Chloe Roth, Chloe Stewart, Chloe Veltman,

Chris Aschauer, Chris Baum, Chris Campbell, Chris Chon, Chris Cobb, Chris Drakeford, Chris Fan, Chris Fitzpatrick, Chris Freimuth, Chris Gerben, Chris Hammer, Chris Harrington, Chris Haworth, Chris Holt, Chris Lele, Chris Mackay, Chris Parker, Chris Reade, Chris Roberts, Chris Ryan, Chris Taylor, Chris Tillisch, Chris Tong, Chris Warner, Chris Westfal, Chris Wrede, Chris Ying, Chrissy Loader, Christal Yuen, Christell Asken, Christell Askew, Christian Montalvo, Christie Maliyackel, Christina Amini, Christina Biodini, Christina Camano, Christina Dickinson, Christina Empedodes, Christina Endres, Christina Frank, Christina Jovanelly, Christina Kelso, Christina Kerby, Christina Manalansan, Christina Needham, Christina Park, Christina Fawn Lee, Christina Richardson, Christina Ruiz-Esparza, Christina Whalen, Christina Wu, Christina Yang, Christina Zentmyer, Christine Cathcart, Christine Chu, Christine Cordner, Christine Dibiasi, Christine Giordano, Christine Hendrickson, Christine Parkins, Christine Saddul, Christine Shim, Christine Steel, Christine Tarn, Christine Whalen, Christopher Benz, Christopher Bloomfield, Christopher Cobb, Christopher Cook, Christopher Cullen, Christopher Danner, Christopher Hall, Christopher Hemond, Christopher Holmes, Christopher Nelson, Christopher Worrall, Christopher Hermelin, Christopher Ying, Christy Chan, Christoper Kerscher, Christy Higgins, Christy Meyer, Christy Susman, Cicely Sweed, Cindy Brinkman, Cindy David, Cindy Ehrlich, Cindy Merrick, Clae Styron, Claire Bain, Claire Becker, Claire Bloomberg, Claire Conway, Claire Diepenbrock, Claire Doran, Claire Greenwood, Claire Hoffman, Claire Murdough, Claire Padilla, Claire Powell, Claire Rawlins, Claire Salinda, Claire Sherba, Clare Jacobson, Clare Perry, Clare Szydlowski, Clarissa Buck, Claudia Bermudez, Claudia Bluhm, Claudia Bushee, Claudia Trotch, Claudine Asbagh, Claudine Ibrahim, Clifford Jay Bell, Clifford Stanley, Clint Sallee, Coby McDonald, Coco Jones, Cody Reiss, Coe Leta Stratford, Colby Lind, Colin Blake, Colin Casey, Colin Dabkowski, Colin Dobrowski, Colin Hector, Colin Murray, Colin Murphy, Colin Sullivan, Colleen Bazdarich, Colleen Burke-Pitts, Colleen Cotter, Colleen Lloyd, Colleen McVearry, Colleen O'Connor, Collins Tao, Conan Knoll, Conan Liu, Conan Putnam, Connie Rubiano, Connor Buestad, Conrad Newman, Constanza Svidler, Cora Stuyker, Corey Wade, Cori Miller, Corianne Brosnahan, Corrine Cadon, Corina Carrasco, Corina Derman, Corinne Goria, Cortney McDevitt, Cortney Rickman-Green, Cory Banks, Cory Doctorow, Cory Nelson, Courtney Dillon, Courtney Germain, Courtney Ham, Courtney Landis, Craig Butz, Craig Charney, Craig Charnley, Craig Kelly, Craig Lloyd, Craig Phillips, Crispin Boxer, Cristal Guderjahn, Cristal Java, Cristina Deptula, Cristina Giner, Crossley Pinkstaff, Crystal Karabelas, Crystal Smith, Crystal Yang, Curtis F. Walters, Cynthia Chavez, Cynthia McAfee, Cynthia Nguyen, Cynthia Popper, Cynthia Poster, Cynthia Robinson, Cynthia Shannon, Cyrus Philbrick, Dae Houlihan, Dae Woo Son, Daglish Chew, Dagny Dingman, Daisy Eneix, Dakota Kim, Dale Hoyt, Dalia Regos, Damien English, Damon Robertson, Dan Archer, Dan Edelstein, Dan Finnegan, Dan Gingold, Dan Kaufman, Dan Liberthson, Dan McHale, Dan Miranda, Dan Nied, Dan Schaefer, Dan Strachota, Dan Sullivan, Dan Turner, Dan Verel, Dan Weatherfield-Lichtenberg, Dana Arnold, Dana Beatty, Dana Carmody-Burns, Dana Comiskey, Dana Cunningham, Dana Moe Halley, Dana Isokawa, Dana Katz, Dana Nguyen, Dana Sacchetti, Dana Schmidt, Dana Yobst, Dana Zullo, Dane Olmstead, Dani

McClain, Danica Suskin, Daniel "Danny" Habib, Daniel Alarcon, Daniel
Biewener, Daniel Brownstein, Daniel Canestaro-Garcia, Daniel Fee, Daniel
Galicia, Daniel Glendening, Daniel Gumbiner, Daniel Handler, Daniel Homer,
Daniel Peixoto Irby, Daniel Kimerling, Daniel Miller, Daniel Mulkin, Daniel
Raskin, Daniel Schcolnik, Daniel Sheltzer, Daniel Song, Daniel Uchiyama, Daniel
Velazquez, Daniel Weiss, Daniel White, Daniel Worden, Daniel Yadegar, Daniela
Bazán, Daniela Delvos, Daniella Beznicki, Danielle DiAngelo, Danielle
Richardson, Danielle Vieth, Danielle Von Lehman, Danielle Wayne, Danika
Maddocks, Danni Biondini, Danni Fruehe, Danny Lin, Danny Torres, Dantia
MacDonald, Dara Colwell, Dara Kosberg, Darcy Asbe, Darcy Morris, Darelene
Aloot, Daria Portillo, Darren Dieguez, Darren Franich, Darren Morgan, Darryl
Forman, Dave Donofrio, Dave Eggers, Dave Friedman, Dave Giesen, Dave
Richmond, Dave Shlachter, Davi Marra, David Adams, David Atlas, David
Beaulieu, David Becker, David Beisly-Guiotto, David Berends, David Bill, David
Brown, David Brownell, David Calbert, David Card, David Cheng, David Chow,
David Cole, David Cole, David Corbett, David Ewald, David Fedman, David Fein,
David Galvez, David Grefrath, David Johnson Jr, David Johnson-Igra, David
Johnston, David Ka Wai Pan, David Katznelson, David Klein, David Looby, David
Marx, David Murphy, David Petzold, David Richardson, David Shultz, David
Soleimani-Meigooni, David Spero, David Stager, David I. Steinberg, David Steuer,
David Stockhausen, David Teitel, David Thal, David Trovato, David Wooll, David
Wygant, David Young, Dawn Marie Knopf, Dayna Shaw, Dean Civitello, Deanna
Reardon, Deb Farkas, Debbi Reinschmiedt, Debbie Goldstein, Debbie Hampton,
Debbie Huey, Debbie Kang, Debbie Ken, Debbie Moguillansky, Debbie
Steingesser, Debbie Weinberg, Deborah Bernard, Deborah Chilvers, Deborah
England, Deborah Fedorchuk, Deborah Kirk, Deborah Kitchens, Deborah Wade
Matheson, Deborah Nagle-Burke, Deborah Schatten, Debra Berliner, Debra
Glass, Debra Hannula, Debra Schutz, Deena Arnanoff, Deirdre Costello, Denis
Higginbotham, Denise Chiang, Denise Dooley, Denise Esteves, Denise Hill,
Denise Marcia, Denise Padilla, Denise Sauerteig, Dennis Creagh, Dennis Dizon,
Dennis Evans, Dennis Lu, Denny Palmer, Derek Fagerstrom, Derek Garnett,
Derek Jackson, Deric Brown, Devi Kane Zinzuvadia, Devin Asaro, Devin Davis,
Devin Spicer, Devon Beddard, Devon Bella, Devon Fitzgerald, Devorah Lauter,
Dewey Hammond, Diana Barclay, Diana Iakoubova, Diana Lemberg, Diana
Mangaser, Diana Martinez, Diana Perez, Diana Peters, Diana Reardon, Diana
Sailer, Diana Shook, Diane Barghouthy, Diane Campese, Diane Durst, Dianne
Gallo, Dietz Isaac, Dilaria Parry, Dina Hirsch, Dina Marshalek, Dina Pugh, Dina
Wilson, Dmitry Shevelenko, Dmitriy Shirchenko, Dodie Han, Dominic Luxford,
Dominica Kriz, Dominique Morrison, Dominque Bayart, Don George, Donald
Francis Jr., Donald Jans, Donald Tetto, Donaldo Prescod, Donna Lack, Donna
Levreault, Donna Williamson, Dorinda von Stroheim, Doris Owyang, Dorothy
Joo, Dory Ellis, Doug Favero, Doug Hawkins, Doug Henderson, Doug Lawrence,
Doug Offenhartz, Doug Wilkins, Douglas Borchert, Douglas Dowers, Douglas Fox,
Douglas Gray, Douglas MacMillan, Douglas McGray, Dovid Krafchow, Doyle Ed
Bell Jr., Drew Marshall, Drew Roesch-Knapp, Dustin Delaney, Dustin Johnston,
Dusty Neu, Dusty Stokes, Dwayne Swanson, Dylan Houle, Dylan Tokar, Dylan
Twcney, Dylan Wooters, E.K. Keith, Earnest Cardenas, Ed Yoon, Eddie Ahn, Edie

Dagley, Edith Fox, Edward Calhoun, Edward Opton, Edwin Loeza, Eileen Roche, Elaina Acosta-Ford, Elaine Beale, Elaine Lee, Elaine Ng, Elaine Walker, Elana Aoyman, Elana Roston, Eleanor Brockman, Eleanor Sananman, Elena Coco, Elena Mulroney, Elena Shapiro, Elexa Poropudas, Eli Altman, Eli Horowitz, Eli Sheridan, Eli Steffen, Eli Wald, Elijah Carroll, Elinor Smith, Elisabeth Karlin Wagstaffe, Elisabeth "Beth" Miles, Elise Allen, Elise Craig, Elise Heilbrunn, Elissa Bassist, Elissa Calvin, Elissa Hamlat, Elizabeth Anne Convery, Elizabeth Bernstein, Elizabeth Cabral, Elizabeth Cohon, Elizabeth Davidson, Elizabeth "Beth" Duddy, Elizabeth Dunn, Elizabeth Easton, Elizabeth Engellenner, Elizabeth Esfahani, Elizabeth Gadbaw, Elizabeth Gannes, Elizabeth Hamilton-Guarino, Elizabeth Hille, Elizabeth Hillman, Elizabeth Hodder, Elizabeth Hodder, Elizabeth Hoody, Elizabeth Hurt, Elizabeth "Zil" Jaeger, Elizabeth Keenley, Elizabeth Kennedy, Elizabeth Kert, Elizabeth Kohout, Elizabeth Maki, Elizabeth "Libby" Molina, Elizabeth Montalbano, Elizabeth Moore, Elizabeth Nichols, Elizabeth Nordlinger, Elizabeth Parker, Elizabeth Santiago, Elizabeth Saviano, Elizabeth Shafer, Elizabeth Sigler, Elizabeth Lesly Stevens, Elizabeth Switaj, Elizabeth Toole, Elizabeth Vereker, Elizabeth Wake, Elizabeth West, Elizabeth Winter, Elizabeth Zambelli, Elka Weber, Ella Lawrence, Ellen Atkinson, Ellen Berman, Ellen Beall Dubreuil, Ellen Ellen Goodenow, Ellen Halter, Ellen Harding, Ellen Hoener, Ellen Hornstein, Ellen Johnson, Brooke Lee, Ellen Mulligan, Ellen Scarpaci, Ellen Sherman, Ellen Veen, Elline Farley, Elline Lipkin, Elliot Harmon, Elliot Onn, Elliott Gluck, Ellyn Rosenthal, Elyse Bekins, Elyse Lightman, Em Warren, Emberly Nesbitt, Emi Kojima, Emile Baizel, Emilia Varshavsky, Emiliano Huet-Vaughn, Emilie Noble, Emily Berger, Emily Blankinship, Emily Bruenig, Emily Cohen, Emily Colman, Emily Daugherty, Emily Davis, Emily Dreyfuss, Emily Drobny, Emily Erlendson, Emily Fasten, Emily Finkel, Emily Fleet, Emily Goligoski, Emily Hughes, Emily Janzer, Emily Jocson, Emily Juarez, Emily Katz, Emily Kirkland, Emily Liebowitz, Emily Lowe, Emily Macy, Emily Marsh, Emily Moore, Emily Oestreicher, Emily Ostendorf, Emily Parker, Emily Peck, Emily Satterstrom, Emily Sims, Emily Taylor-Mortorff, Emily Teitsworth, Emily Tyler, Emily Van Duyne, Emily Virgil, Emily Watkins, Emily Wentz, Emily Wilkerson, Emily Windsor, Emma Collier, Emma Dunbar, Emma Ellis, Emma Hewitt, Emma Silvers, Emma Vuletic, Emma Williams, Emma Zevin, Emmanuel Darzins, Enrique Gonzales, Epi Arias, Eric Bankston, Eric Barry, Eric Cetnarski, Eric Dumbleton, Eric Edgeworth, Eric Hellweg, Eric Hoffman, Eric Larson, Eric Magnuson, Eric Meltzer, Eric Molina, Eric Nguyen, Eric Prejean, Eric Rowe, Eric Schaible, Eric Simons, Eric Slatkin, Eric Spitznagel, Eric Sullivan, Eric Tipler, Eric Valenzuela, Eric Wilinski, Erica Brown, Erica Blumenson-Cook, Erica Chien, Erica Dreisbach, Erica Friday, Erica Hadden, Erica Lewis, Erica Martz, Erica Martz, Erica Roe, Erica Scheidt, Erica Toews, Erich Matthes, Erik Joule, Erik Michaels-Ober, Erik Pankonin, Erik Totten, Erik Vance, Erika Brekke, Erika Lewis, Erika Mielke, Erika Young, Erin Archer, Erin Archuleta, Erin Augustine, Erin Blanton, Erin Bregman, Erin Clarke, Erin Cornelius, Erin Dorn, Erin Dougherty, Erin Gulbengay, Erin Hyman, Erin Jourdan, Erin Kuka, Erin Kuschner, Erin Lindberg, Erin Milgram, Erin Potts, Erin Roth, Erin Sherbert, Erin Tao, Erin Traylor, Erin Wilkey, Erin Winters, Erin Zimmer, Erinn Hatter, Ernie Calderon, Ernie Hsiung, Esme Shaller, Esther

Cervantes, Esther Lee, Ethan Watters, Eugenia Chan, Eugenia Chien, Eugenie Howard-Johnston, Eun-Jong Lee, Eunice Kang, Eva Allred, Eva Chao, Eva Dienel, Eva Sherertz, Evalyn Carmack, Evalyne Michaut, Evan Babb, Evan Chase, Evan Doll, Evan Graner, Evan Huggins, Evan Kennedy, Evan Kinkel, Evan Lenoir, Evan Wiig, Evan Wynns, Evany Thomas, Eve Ekman, Eve O'Neill, Eve Pell, Evelyn Krampf, Evi Steyer, Evin Wolverton, Ewlin Cotman, Ezra Kwong, Faith McGee, Faith Songco, Fauzia Musa, Felicity Harrold, Felicity Rose, Felix Chow, Felix M. Chow, Fergusson Assaf, Fernando "Danny" Hidalgo, Filip Muki Dobeanic, Filip Kesler, Florence Ion, Flynn De Marco, Frances Lefkowitz, Frances Stroh, Frances Whitnall, Francie King, Francis Whitenhall, Frank Holland, Francisco Mora, Frank Lee, Frank Marquardt, Frank Molina, Fransiska Santana, Frederick Mead, Frederick Osborn, Fredric Silverman, Gabe Roth, Gabe Weisert, Gabriel Derita, Gabriel Francis, Gabriel Kram, Gabriel Roth, Gabriel Trionfi, Gabriela Hernandez, Gabrielle Falzone, Gabrielle Goodbar, Gabrielle Messineo, Gabrielle Toft, Gaby DiMuro, Gahl Shottan, Gail Jardine, Galen Leach, Galen Leach, Gami Haynes, Garen Torikian, Garrett Kamps, Garrett Loube, Gary Gach, Gary Gooch, Gary Jones, Gary Moskowitz, Gary Sloboda, Gaston Lau, Gayle Keck, Gayle Leyton, Geeta Dharmappa, Gemma Velasquez, Geneva Lovett, Genevieve Compton, Genevieve Robertson, Genevieve Wallace, Genine Lentine, Gennesis Gastilo, Geoff Gallinger, Geoff Libby, Geoff Schwarten, Geoffrey Libby, George Chem, George Chen, George Cotsirilos, George Davis, George Shultz, Georgie Devereux, Gerald Ambinder, Gerard Jones, Geri Ehle, Gerin River, Gerry Moriorty, Gheanna Emelia, Gianmama Franchini, Gianmarco Savio, Gianmaria Franchim, Gianmaria Francini, Gibson Verkuil, Gil Stoltz, Gillian Croen, Gillian Masland, Gina Abellkop, Gina Balibrera, Gina Donohoe, Gina Rivera, Gina Welch, Ginevra Kirkland, Giselle Shardlow, Glenda Bautista, Glendon Roy, Glenn Kelman, Gloria Charry, Gloria Lenhart, Glory Leilani Ludwick, Gloria Son, Gordon Smith, Grace Klein, Grace Loh, Grace Rubenstein, Grace Schlesinger, Grace Smith, Grace Wong, Grace Sherry Wong, Gracie Dulik, Gracie Robinson, Grant Kerber, Graig Butz, Grayson Stebbins, Greg Bickel, Greg De Pascale, Greg Dubrow, Greg Dubrow, Greg Fitzsimmons, Greg Powell, Greg Rasmussen, Greg Wiercioch, Gregory Crouch, Gregory Loome, Greta Lorge, Greta Mittner, Greta Weiss, Greta Weiss, Gretchen Lang, Gretchen Puttkamer, Gretchen Weber, Griffin Clark, Guity Froz, Gustavo, Guy Brookshire, Hacker Kelli, Hadi Karsoho, Hadley Barrett, Hadley Northrop, Hadley Suter, Hai Huang, Haley Fauth, Haley Pelton, Haley Stocking, Hallina Popko, Halsey Chait, Hagar Kantor, Hana Hammer, Hanif O'Neil, Hank Holzgrefe III, Hank Hozgrefe, Hannah Copperman, Hannah Darling, Hannah Foster, Hannah Ingram, Hannah Mae Blaire, Hannah Schilperoot, Hans Berggren, Hansa Shah, Hansa Shah, Harold Check, Harold Stusnick, Harris Loeser, Harvey Rabbit, Heather Antonissen, Heather Blish, Heather Campbell, Heather Cullen, Heather Gates, Heather Gold, Heather Gunderman, Heather Hax, Heather Hough, Heather Jones, Heather Mack, Heather McMurphy, Heather McNabb, Heather Murphy, Heather O'Neill, Heather Pez, Heather Rasley, Heather Rosner, Heather Smith, Heather Tenney, Heather Terrell, Heather Tidgewell, Heather Turbeville, Heather Vander Zwaag, Heather White, Heidi Erbe, Heidi Fridricksson, Hedi Saraf, Heidi Schmidt, Helaine Melnitzer, Helen de Give, Helen Friedman, Helen Ghaibeh, Helen Parker,

Helena Keeffe, Henry Chan, Henry Goldman, Henry Jones, Henry Murphy, Herman Wong, Hershey Dominick, Hideki Brian Ito, Hilary Abramson, Hilary Hoynes, Hilary Lawson, Hilary Merril, Hilary Rubicam-Merrill, Hiya Swanhoyser, Holly Grigg-Spall, Holly Hale, Holly McDede, Howard Harband, Hsonia Arteaga, Hugh Biggar, Hunter Lydon, Iain Johnston, Ian Carruthers, Ian Carulthers, Ian Evans, Ian Fink, Ian Hart, Ian Clardino, Ian McKellar, Ian Port, Ian Singleton, Ian Stewart, Ianna Hawkins Owen, Ie-chen Cheng, Iga Kozlowski, Ilana Bain, Ileana Shelvin, Ilene Ivins, Ilona M. Fox, Ilyse Opas, Imran Zaidi, Ina Acuña, India Leigh, Inez Machado, Ingrid Hawkinson, Ingrid Keir, Inna Arzumanova, Inna Volynskaya, Irene Moore, Irene Moosen, Irene Yoon, Irina Zeylikovich, Iriss Clymer, Irissa Everett, Irit Schneider, Isaac Constantine, Isaac Ebersole, Isabel Miller-Bottome, Isadora Epstein, Issac Ebersole, Ivie English, Izabel Arnold, Jacinta Cruz, Jack Bouleware, Jack Carlson, Jack Chang, Jack Hanlon, Jack McClane, Jack Muse, JacRita Mare Sapunor, Jack Nixon • Jack Shafer • Jack Wranovics • Jackie Bello • Jackson Losh • Jackson West • Jaclyn Shanahan • Jacob Bromberg • Jacob Kramer • Jacob Leland • Jacob Muran • Jacqueline Davidson • Jacqueline Wallace • Jacqui Ipp • Jacqui Shine • Jade Brooks • Jae Kang • Jaime Adrian • Jaime Davila • Jaime Hammond • Jamie Lanin • Jamie Lundy • Jaime Munger • Jaime Ordonez Centeno • Jaimee Rungsitiyakorn • Jake Chapnick • Jake Swearingen • James Brooke • James Calder • James Cotter • James Dekker • James DeKoven • James Dockeray • James Holt • James Kinsman • James Martin • James Newburg • James O'Donnell • James Rocchi • James Scheibli • James Warner • James Weckler • James Williams • Jamie Flam • Jamie Francisco • Jamie Hand • Jamie Johnston • Jamie Marron • Jamie Wong • Jamilah King • Jane Flint • Jane Francis • Jane Ganahl • Jane Goldsmith • Jane Guzzo • Jane Partensky • Jane Rauckhorst • Jane Scheppke • Jane St. John • Jane Yin • Jane Yu • Janet Ference • Janet Yu • Janice Greene • Janice Lobo Sapigao • Janice Smith • Janine Bryan • Janine Mogannam • Janis Cosor • Jano Cortijo • Jaqui Ipp • Jared Frazer • Jared Holst • Jared Horney • Jared Maliga • Jared Renfro • Jared Schwartz • Jarrie Chang • Jason Turbow • Jason Biehl • Jason Blakley • Jason Dane • Jason Fager • Jason Flatowicz • Jason Ford • Jason Galeon • Jason Hair • Jason Hilford • Jason H. Hoag • Jason Hofmann • Jason Moiseyev • Jason Qin • Jason Roberts • Jason Thompson • Jason Winshell • Jason Yelvington • Jasper Jackson-Gleich • Javier Daniel Bermudez Garcia • Javier Heinz • Jay Kang • Jayne Lyn Stahl • Jay Taber • Jay Werber • Jaynel Attolini • Jaynie Healy • JayShy Shshsmullington • Jean Allan • Jean Foster • Jean Han • Jeanette Park • Jeanie Hunt-Gibbon • Jeanine Thorpe • Jeanmarie Donovan • Jeanne Beacom • Jeanne Feuerstein • Jeanne Storck • Jeannie Choi • Jeannie Cruz • Jeannine Stickle • Jed Fenchel • Jeff Castle • Jeff Dal Cerro • Jeff Elliott • Jeff Ferguson • Jeff Land • Jeff Lyon • Jeff Mitchell • Jeff Murphy • Jeff Nardinelli • Jeff O'Leary • Jeff Phillips • Jeff Sher • Jeff Stevenson • Jeff Stryker • Jeff Walker • Jeffrey Edalatpour • Jeffrey Guarrera • Jeffrey Halter • Jeffrey Johnson • Jeffrey Knutson • Jeffrey Milum • Jeffrey Porter • Jeffrey Whitehead • Jeffrey Wright • Jemma Lorenat • Jemma Love • Jen Berg • Jen Gann • Jen Loman • Jen O'Neal • Jen Pitts • Jen Rios • Jen Siraganian • Jen Tartaglione • Jen Wan • Jen Wang • Jenee LeMarque • Jeni Johnson • Jeni Paltiel • Jenifer Maravillas • Jenn Mar • Jenn Pries • Jenn Tickes • Jenna Lane • Jennie Larson • Jennie-Marie Adler • Jennifer Anthony • Jennifer Appenrodt • Jennifer Bennett • Jennifer Birch • Jennifer Blackwell • Jennifer Boriss • Jennifer Brandl •

Jennifer Bunshoft • Jennifer Carlson • Jennifer Chien • Jennifer Cho • Jennifer Chu •
Jennifer Clare • Jennifer Daly • Jennifer Feng • Jennifer Fleisher • Jennifer Frances •
Jennifer Frank • Jennifer Frudden • Jennifer Gamez • Jennifer Hahn • Jennifer Hillner
• Jennifer Jackson • Jennifer Jahahnh • Jennifer Jeffrey • Jennifer Kagel • Jennifer
Kain • Jennifer King • Jennifer Lane • Jennifer Lee • Jennifer Lewis • Jennifer Lin •
Jennifer Lindstedt • Jennifer Ling • Jennifer Lipscomb • Jennifer Marston • Jennifer
Massoni • Jennifer "Lulu" McAllister • Jennifer Moffitt • Jennifer Morton • Jennifer
Nedeau • Jennifer Nellis • Jennifer Ng • Jennifer Nickel • Jennifer Patel • Jennifer
Petke • Jennifer Polishook • Jennifer Reczkowski • Jennifer Reiley • Jennifer Reimer
• Jennifer Saltmarsh • Jennifer Saura • Jennifer Schwartz • Jennifer Sembera •
Jennifer Sloan • Jennifer Small • Jennifer Smith • Jennifer Soffen • Jennifer Tanguay
• Jennifer Terrill • Jennifer Thompson • Jennifer Traig • Jennifer Van Hove • Jennifer
Wells • Jennifer Wilks • Jennifer Wokaty • Jennifer Yao • Jenny Argueta • Jenny
Bitner • Jenny Chin Yee Mar • Jenny Doyle • Jenny Glennon • Jenny Greenburg •
Jenny Lovold • Jenny Phu • Jenny Traig • Jenny Wu • Jenny Zhang • Jeremey Lavoi
• Jeremiah Church • Jeremiah Turner • Jeremy Bates • Jeremy Campbell • Jeremy
Gershen • Jeremy Novy • Jeremy Padow • Jeremy Schevling • Jeremy Schneider •
Jeremy Tarr • Jerome Fox • Jerome Martinez • Jerry Steiner • Jess Gill • Jess Granger
• Jess Wells • Jess Wendover • Jessa Loomis • Jesse Coburn • Jesse Eisenhower • Jesse
Eschenroeder • Jesse Fox • Jesse Gillispie • Jesse Lichtenstein • Jesse Misslin • Jesse
Moore • Jesse Rhodes • Jesse Steinchen • Jesse Wilkins • Jesse Young • Jessia Jarjoura
• Jessica Arndt • Jessica Beard • Jessica Binder • Jessica Char • Jessica Chrastil •
Jessica Conrad • Jessica Curiale • Jessica Dur • Jessica Fleischman • Jessica Gage •
Jessica Goldman • Jessica Hansen • Jessica Hemerly • Jessica Jardine • Jessica
Jarjoura • Jessica Kahn • Jessica Langlois • Jessica Lansdon • Jessica Larsen • Jessica
Lobl • Jessica Misslin • Jessica Mordo • Jessica Partch • Jessica Pierce • Jessica Quick
• Jessica Richman • Jessica Server • Jessica Sheehan • Jessica Teisher • Jessica Tzur
• Jessica von Brachel • Jessica Walter • Jessica Washburn • Jessica Weikers • Jessica
Williams • Jessica Wright • Jessica Yurkofsky • Jessie Char • Jessie Churchill • Jessika
Fruchter • Jesús Osuna • Jill Anderson • Jill Bergantz • Jill Dovale • Jill Richardson •
Jill Schinberg • Jill Stauffer • Jill Tomasetti • Jillian Collins • Jim Beckmeyer • Jim
Brook • Jim Dycus • Jim Greer • Jim Mannix • Jim McCaffrey • Jim Patterson • Jim
Wang • Jim Yagmin • Jina Park • Jo Ann Brothers • Joan Gelfand • JoAnn Koga •
Joanna Locke • Joanna Bloomfield • Joanna Calo • Joanna Fax • Joanna Green •
Joanna McNaney • Joanna Normoyle • Joanna Sokolowski • Joanne Long • Joanne
Parsont • Joanne Sterbentz • Joanne Stevens • Jocelyn Becherer • Jody Worthington
• Joe Brown • Joe Conway • Joe Manning • Joe Mud • Joe Ramelo • Joe Rieke • Joe
Wi • Joel Aurora • Joel Brown • Joel Krauska • Joel Richards • Joen Madonna • Joey
Deschenes • Joey McGarvey • Joey Samaniego • Joey Stevenson • Joey Sweet •
Johanna Poch • John Aranda • John Blanco • John Borland • John Brice • John Collins
• John Cornwell • John Daigre • John Douglass • John Flinn • John Foster • John
Garrison • John Garvie • John Gibler • John Kane • John Kim • John Lee • John
Maxey • John McAllister • John McDonald • John "Riley" McLaughlin • John
McMurtrie • John Melvin • John Morrison • John Reed • John Rosenzweig • John
Salvo • John Scopelleti • John Shon • John Snyder • John Sousa • John Theisen • John
Washington • Johnathan Travis • Johnathan Winawer • Johnny Stafford • Jon Boilard
• Jon Kiefer • Jon Mooallem • Jon Moyer • Jon Skulski • Jon Stenzler • Jon Sung •

Jon Twena • Jon Wynacht • Jonah Hall • Jonathan Adams • Jonathan Austin • Jonathan Basker • Jonathan Burton • Jonathan Callard • Jonathan Dibble • Jonathan Garon • Jonathan Hirsch • Jonathan Maiullo • Jonathan Mayer • Jonathan McLeod • Jonathan Rosen • Jonathan Ruthazer • Jonathan Shekter • Jonathan Siker • Jonathan Trunnel • Jonathan White • Jonathan Zuk • Jonathon Hayes • Jonathon McLeod • Joni Blecher • Jono Finger • Joohee Muromcew • Jordan Graham • Jordan Kobert • Jordan Levantini • Jordan Matheny • Jorge Cino • Jorge Medrano • Jory John • Joselyn Nussbaum • Joseph Abello • Joseph Borrelli • Joseph Deschares • Joseph Diaz • Joeseph Ferrell • Joseph Galante • Joseph Remick • Josephine Hill • Josh Green • Josh Greene • Josh Heidemen • Josh Levitz • Josh Rojas • Josh Sisco • Josh Slobin • Joshua Caraco • Joshua Drew • Joshua Gustafson • Joshua Kamler • Joshua Nguyen • Joshua Siegel • Joshua Snyder • Joshua Wein • Joslyn Hamilton • Josslyn Mikow • Josu Garmendia • Joy Kim • Joyce Feuille • Joyce Lin-Conrad • Jr. Daeschner • Juan Alvarado • Juan Matarese • Judi Linn • Judith Jordan • Judith Rolleri • Judy DeMocker • Judy Liao • Judy Wang • Judy Wiatrek Trum • Julia Darcey • Julia Doyle • Julia Grebenstein • Julia Kibben • Julia Meuse • Julia Parmer • Julia Robinson • Julia Smith • Julia Torti • Julia Vinyard • Julia Wai • Julia Westhoff • Juliana Cammarata • Juliana Sloane • Julianne Hing • Julianne Balmain • Julie Ahlbrandt • Julie Chang • Julie Chanter • Julie Conquest • Julie Davis • Julie Dyer • Julie Fishkin • Julie Freeman • Julie Guo • Julie Hassen • Julie Landry-Petersen • Julie Mackay • Julie Mayhew • Julie Mitchell • Julie Pham • Julie Racioppo • Julie Rehmeyer • Julie Salvi • Julie Sims • Julie Sloane • Julie Wagne • Julie Wallerstedt • Julie Wurm • Julienne Gherardi • Juliette Berg • June Jackson • June McKay • Justin Bagnall • Justin Berthelsen • Justin Carder • Justin Gabaldon • Justin Haugh • Justin Honegger • Justin Housman • Justin Hughes • Justin Lamb • Justin Lorentz • Justin Smith • Justin Torkelson • Justine Hebron • Justine Juson • Kailin Clarke • Kaitlin Magoon • Kaitlyn Dunn • Kaitlyn Geremia • Kaitlyn Ortberg • Kaitlyn Rorke • Kaizar Campwala • Kaleena Stoddard • Kali Eichen • Kalyan Meegada • Kammy Lee • Kanwalropp Singh • Kara Cooperrider • Kara Hinman • Kara Krumpe • Kara Stefanidis • Kara Swisher • Karen Allen • Karen Ansel • Karen Duffin • Karen Lichtenberg • Karen Macklin • Karen Regelman • Karen Schaser • Kari Hatch • Karim Quecada Khoury • Karin Elena Orr • Karin Visnick • Karl Langer • Karla Anne Merino Nielsen • Karline Mclain • Karly Sherwood • Karma Bennett • Kasia Cieplak-Mayr von Baldegg • Katarina Ana Milicevic • Kate Aiken • Kate Anderson • Kate Bueler • Kate Catanese • Kate Dollarhyde • Kate Dunphy • Kate Elston • Kate Folk • Kate Gagnon • Kate Goldstein-Breyer • Kate Kokontis • Kate Kudirka • Kate Marshall • Kate Marvel • Kate McDonough • Kate Nicolai • Kate Pavao • Kate Schox • Kate Sweeney • Kate Torgersen • Kate Viernes • Kate Wahl • Katelyn St. John • Katerhine Robb • Katerine Bruens • Katharine Lu • Katharine Morris • Katharine Painter • Katharine Sontag • Katharine Tom • Katherine Alissa Harrison-Adcock • Katherine Casey • Katherine Covell • Katherine Emery • Katherine Joseph • Katherine Krause • Katherine Kugay • Katherine McCarthy • Katherine Morris • Katherine Nelson • Katherine Rochemont • Katherine Swan • Katherine Tillotson • Katherine Tom • Kathleen Arnolds • Kathleen Bertolani • Kathleen Cohn • Kathleen Dodge • Kathleen Haley • Kathleen Hennessy • Kathleen Miller • Kathleen Morgan • Kathrina Manalac • Kathryn Bertram • Kathryn Hopping • Kathryn Keslosky • Kathryn Lavin • Kathryn Olney • Kathryn Zupsick • Kathy Cantrell • Kathy Chong • Kathy Garlick • Kathy

Mandry Cohn • Katia Noyes • Katie Bailey • Katie Boehnlein • Katie Bouch • Katie
Bradley • Katie Burke • Katie Carter • Katie Crouch • Katie Dunbar • Katie Edmonds
• Katie Fahey • Katie Farnsworth • Katie Fowley • Katie Fraser • Katie Gray • Katie
Henry • Katie Herman • Katie Hintz • Katie Hoffman • Katie Hughes • Katie Kuhl •
Katie MacLean • Katie Mayo • Katie Minks • Katie Mitchell • Katie Moore • Katie
Pfeiffer • Katie Prenda • Katie Reeves • Katie Richardson • Katie Warren • Katie
Westbrook • Katina Papson • Katrina Dodson • Katrina Markel • Katrina Wagner •
Katy Crenshaw • Katy Hunt • Kayla Kristine Grimm • Kazz Regelman • Keane Li •
Keef Ward • Keegan Finberg • Keely Nunez • Keith Knight • Keith Spencer • Keith
Riegert • Keith Tanner • Kelci Lucier • Kelli Bratvold • Kellie Schmitt • Kelly Booth
• Kelly Buchanan • Kelly Gemmill • Kelly Hendricks • Kelly Johnson • Kelly Kulsrud
• Kelly Luce • Kelly Nuxoll • Kelly Osmundson • Kelly Osterling • Kelly Phipps •
Kelly Pretzer • Kelly Rae McLachlan • Kelly Stewart • Kelsey Parker • Kelsey
Siggins • Kelson Kwong • Ken Ensslin • Ken Martin • Ken Reisman • Ken Yee •
Kendra Terry • Kendyll Pappas • Kenneth Goldberg • Kenneth Lau • Kenneth Traynor
• Kenneth Yuan • Kenton Kivestu • Kenwyn Derby • Kenya Lewis • Keren Ackerman
• Keren Kama • Keri Modrall • Keri Shawn • Kerri Arsenault • Kerry Fleisher • Kerry
Suzanne Kyle • Kerry Lee • Kerry Ratza • Kerry Smith • Kevin Adams • Kevin
Bayley • Kevin Buckelew • Kevin Christopher • Kevin Cline • Kevin Coleman •
Kevin Collier • Kevin Cummins • Kevin Ferguson • Kevin Francis • Kevin Grizzard
• Kevin Jones • Kevin Kline • Kevin LaRose • Kevin Lee • Kevin Lingerfelt • Kevin
Luna • Kevin O'Connell • Kevin Redmon • Kevin Rubino • Kevin Sparks • Kevin
Showkat • Kevin Stark • Kevin Woodson • Kevin Zhu • Kian Alavi • Kiara Brinkman
• Kiera Westphal • Kieran Hartsough • Kiersten Stevens • Kikelomo Adedeji • Kiki
Lipsett • Kilmer Gianpaolo • Kim Cooper • Kim Green • Kim Ionesco • Kim Lan •
Kim Rubey • Kim Stuart • Kim-Lan Stadnick • Kimberly Ciszewski • Kimberly
Conley • Kimberly Connor • Kimberly Kim • Kimberly Magowan • Kimberly Wolf
• Kimberly Wyatt • Kinda Nguyen • Kinsley Daniel • Kira Deutch • Kiran Divvela •
Kirsten Webb • Kirstin Ault • Kismet Ragab • Kit Cody • Klover Kim • Kok Lye •
Koren Jones • Kris Pribadi • Krissy Beilke • Krissy Teegerstrom • Krista Canellakis
• Krista Keyes • Krista Klein • Krista Mitzel • Krista Niles • Kristen Cesiro • Kristen
Daniel • Kristen Engelhardt • Kristen Fergot • Kristen Hagn • Kristen Hatcher •
Kristen Hawkinson • Kristen Hren • Kirsten Knight • Kristen Nadaraja • Kristen
Philipkoski • Kristen Poitras • Kristen Schultz Oliver • Kristen Scully • Kristen
Whisenand • Kristen Yawitz • Kristen-Paige Madonia • Kristi Kimball • Kristin Glass
• Kristin Keane • Kristin Pollock • Kristin Tellers • Kristina Buttz • Kristina May
Garrett • Kristina Johnson • Kristina Lewis • Kristina Loring • Kristina Shevory •
Kristina Yee • Kristine Ellis • Kristy Braun • Kristy Phillips • Kristy Red-Horse •
Kritina Clark • Krystina Orozco • Kyla Gibboney • Kyle Anderson • Kyle Griffiths •
Kyle Matthews • Kylen Campbell • Kyveli Diener • Lacee Kine • Lacey Goodloe •
Laila Sovdi • Lailah Robertson • Laine Stranahan • Lalaie Ameeriar • Lan Ngo • Lane
Kennedy • Langdon Moss • Lara Belonogoff • Lara Fox • Larissa Parson • Larry
Habegger • Laura Altieri • Laura Alvarez • Laura Beattie • Laura Brief • Laura Cox •
Laura Darrah • Laura De Palma • Laura Delizonna • Laura Edgar • Laura Fraenza •
Laura French • Laura Hays • Laura Holmes • Laura LeeMoorhead • Laura Lin • Laura
Linden • Laura Lockwood • Laura Maguire • Laura Makinen • Laura Marett • Laura
Mathers • Laura Mazzola • Laura McClure • Laura McKinney • Laura Mesa • Laura

Michelson • Laura Moorhead • Laura Pass • Laura Peach • Laura Ricci • Laura Ross • Laura Rubio • Laura Rumpf • Laura Schadler • Laura Scholes • Laura Simmons • Laura Smyrl • Laura Weiss • Laura Wilson-Tobin • Laura Yaffe • Laura Yamaguchi • Laurel Carman • Laurel Gaddie • Laurel Newby • Lauren Bingham • Lauren Brady • Lauren Bundy • Lauren Byrne • Lauren Chow • Lauren Corden • Lauren de Bruyn • Lauren Eberle • Lauren Entner • Lauren Groff • Lauren Guza • Lauren Hall • Lauren Halsted • Lauren Hamlin • Lauren Hensarling • Lauren Hirshfield • Lauren Hospital • Lauren Khalil • Lauren Ladoceour • Lauren Leabeater • Lauren Lilley • Lauren Markham • Lauren McCauley • Lauren Pellegrino • Lauren Quinn • Lauren Rosenfield • Lauren Ryan • Lauren Sapala • Lauren Toker • Lauren Varner • Lauren Winsor Stenmoe • Laurie Baker-Flynn • Laurie Doyle • Laurie Robinson • Laurie Weed • Lavinia Spalding • Lawrence Schear • Lea Erinberg • Leah Bowers • Leah Brucker • Leah Fergenson • Leah Lader • Leah Weiss • Leah Welborn • Leanne Vanderbyl • Lee Henderson • Lee Granas • Lee Howard • Lee Jensen • Lee Konstantinou • Leena Brisch • Leena Prasad • Leia Asanuma • Leida Schoggen • Leif Isaksen • Leigh Lucas • Leigh Roxas • Leila Carrillo • Leila Easa • Leila Hamidi • Leland Cheuk • Lena Zúñiga • Leon Yu • Leonard Cetrangolo • Leora Broydo Vestel • Leora Harling • Lesley Quinn • Lesley Stample • Leslie Absher • Leslie Bahr • Leslie Brown • Leslie Coles • Leslie Cranford • Leslie Engle • Leslie Guttman • Leslie Hamanaka • Leslie Henkel • Leslie Jamison • Leslie Kelly • Leslie Ladow • Leslie Lambert • Leslie Outhier • Leslie Rodd • Leslie Tabor • Lessley Anderson • Leticia Barajas • Leticia Garcia • Lex Leifheit • Lia Killeen • Lia Siebert • Liam Holt • Liam Widman • Liana Holmberg • Liana Small • Liane Yukoff • Lianna Glodt • Libby McMillan • Liberty Velez • Lieva Whitbeck • Lila Stone • Lillie Chilin • Lily Diamond • Lily Mooney • Lily Piyatthaisere • Lily Rosenman • Linda Bott • Linda Chavez • Linda Duck • Linda Gerobe • Linda Goossens • Linda Knox • Linda Lagunas • Linda Puffer • Linda Robertshaw • Linda Tarango • Linda Wilbrecht • Linda Yarlkowsky • Linden Cady • Lindsay Grant • Lindsay Keach • Lindsay Klaestch • Lindsay Mecca • Lindsay Morton • Lindsay Patterson • Lindsay Welch • Lindsey Cookson • Lindsey Goldberg • Lindsey Hultman • Lindsey Keenan • Lindsey Ollman • Lindsey Pace • Linette Escobar • Linnea Ogden • Linnea Newman • Linsey Sandrew • Lis Goldschmidt • Lisa Amick • Lisa Bennett • Lisa Brown • Lisa Davidson • Lisa Degliantoni • Lisa Delgadillo • Lisa Duran • Lisa Friedman • Lisa Gschwandtner • Lisa Heer • Lisa Hom • Lisa Isaacson • Lisa K. Buchanan • Lisa Lee • Lisa Manolius • Lisa Manter • Lisa Morehouse • Lisa Nguyen • Lisa Pearson • Lisa Post • Lisa Presta • Lisa Raffensperger • Lisa Ruff • Lisa Ryers • Lisa Schoonover • Lisa Tauber • Lisa Tharpe • Lisa Webster • Lisa Maria Burkhard • Lissa Rovetch • Lissa Robinson • Listen-Paige Madenia • Liz Bertko • Liz Bort • Liz Dedrick • Liz Haas • Liz Hallock • Liz Hawrylo • Liz Hille • Liz Hollander • Liz Ireland • Liz Johannesen • Liz Kahn • Liz Kelly • Liz Lance • Liz Moore • Liz Nagle • Liz Nolan • Liz Smith • Liz Worthy • Liz Yepsen • Liza Gleason • Liza Sperling • Liza Sweeney • Lizzie Andrews • Lizzie Buchen • Lloyd Cargo • Logan McDowell • Logan Mirto • Logan Shedd • Logan Tribull • Logan Ury • Loran White • Lorelei Trammell • Loren Clemens • Loren Kwan • Loretta Stevens • Lori Burzynski • Lori Cohen • Lori Hostetter • Lori Huskey • Lori Nygaard • Lorian Long • Lorien McKenna • Lorna Walker • Lorraine Cuddeback • Lorraine Honig • Lorraine Lin • Lorrie Wesa • Lou Handler • Lou Moore • Louis "Robert" Alley • Louis Anthes • Louis Gurman • Louise

Lowry • Louise Pon-Barry • Louise Shultz • Louisine Frelinghuysen • Louise Huttinger • Lowen Baumgarten • Lucas Peters • Lucie Hecht • Lucinda Bingham • Lucy Baker • Lucy Herr • Lucy Im • Lucy Ives • Lucy Karanfilian • Lucy Kirchner • Lucy Marton • Lucy O'Leary • Lucy Odling-Smee • Luke Fretwell • Luke Hannafin • Luke Lambert • Luke Sykora • Lulu Orozco • Lydia Pierce • Lynh Ho • Lynn Lent • Lynn Burnett • Lynn Dalsing • Lynn Grogan • Lynne Kaufman • Lynne Roberts • Lyndsey Ellis • Lyndsey Schlax • M. Roshni Ray • Maadhevi Comar • Mac Bennett • Mack Howell • Maddy Russell-Shapiro • Madeleina Halley • Madeleine Anderson • Madeleine Felder • Madeleine Heller • Madeline Clare • Madeline Hansen • Maggie Andrews • Maggie Ballard • Maggie Berry • Maggie Hardy • Maggie Hayes • Maggie Jacobstein • Maggie Ronan • Maggie Sheffer • Maggie Whittington • Maggie Wooll • Maira Baird • Mairead O'Connor • Maiya Reekers • Maja Henderson • Mala Kumar • Malaika Costello-Dougherty • Malena Watrous • Malia Jackson • Malik Konur • Mallory Leone • Mallory Mendelsohn • Mallory Nezam • Mandy McGowen • Manny Silva • Marcella Deproto • Marcia Hofmann • Marcia Rodgers • Marcie Dresbaugh • Marco Loeb • Marco Lopez • Marco Panella • Maren Bean • Maren Nymo • Maren Smith • Margaret Boehme • Margaret Crandall • Margaret Fajarado • Margaret McCarthy • Margaret Smith • Margarita Levantovskaya • Marge Levy • Margi Schierberl • Margo Stern • Margot Jansen • Mari Vargo • Maria Allocco • Maria Alvarellos • Maria Baird • Maria Behan • Maria Boehme • Maria Chacon • Maria De Lorenzo • Maria Hernandez • Maria Jesus Matilla • María José Gonzalez • Maria Kelley • Maria Tattu Bowen • Maria Walcutt • Marianna Cherry • Maria Dichov • Marie Drennan • Marie Glancy • Marie Hamre • Mariko Miki • Marilee Chang Lin • Marilyn Rutz Levy • Mario Bruzzone • Marion Anthonisen • Marisa Armanino • Marisa Hall • Marisa Lagos • Marisa Stertz • Marissa Fernandes • Marissa Hamilton • Marissa Katsuranis • Marissa Korbel • Marjie Graham • Mark Beidelman • Mark Buffo • Mark Cormier • Mark De la Vina • Mark Ewing • Mark Fiore • Mark Follman • Mark Goldberg • Mark Gotelli • Mark Hamilton • Mark Krahling • Mark Krueger • Mark Leonard • Mark Noack • Mark Rabine • Mark Sipowicz • Mark Spolyar • Marko Serpas • Marla Steuer • Marsha Zarco • Marte Osci • Martha Cooley • Martha Grover • Martha Kinney • Martin Nouvell • Marty Castleberg • Mary Banas • Mary Bloom • Mary Bushee • Mary Crofton • Mary Darcy • Mary Davis • Mary Duong • Mary Foyder • Mary Jesionowski • Mary Johnson • Mary Juno • Mary Kolesnikova • Mary Lanham • Mary Murphy • Mary Murphy O'Brien • Mary Petrosky • Mary Rose • Mary S. Russell • Mary Schaefer • Mary Taugher • Mary Warden • Mary Wheelan • Mary Ann Cotter • Mary Ann Malkos • Mary Ann Scheuer • Mary Beth Sacchi • Mary Elaine Akers-Bell • Mary Gail Snyder • Mary Jane Irwin • Mary Kate Cunniff • Marya Grupsmith • Maryanne Rodriguez • Marzia Niccolai • Masha Rumer • Mat Squillante • Mateo Burtch • Mathew Honan • Mathew Morgan • Matt Baxter • Matt Bonar • Matt Chayt • Matt Cooper • Matt Gereghty • Matt Gould • Matt Joyce • Matt Kunzweiler • Matt Laurel • Matt Maenpaa • Matt Middlebrook • Matt Ness • Matt Nester • Matt Parsons • Matt Richtel • Matt Ridella • Matt Runkle • Matt Werner • Matt Wolff • Matt Wheeland • Matthew Allen • Matthew Bell • Matthew Berger • Matthew Borden • Matthew Botticelli • Matthew Ciaschini • Matthew Gomez • Matthew Hein • Matthew Honan • Matthew Kelley • Matthew Keuter • Matthew Lefeel • Matthew Micari • Matthew Morgan • Matthew Olson • Matthew Tabak • Matthew Wolpe • Matthew Yeoman • Matty Merrill • Maura Prendiville • Maureen

Bogues • Maureen Duffy • Maureen Evans • Maureen Sullivan • Maureen Thomas •
Mauro Javier Cardenas • Max Allbee • Max Besbris • Max Farber • Max Frumes •
Max Gertin • Max Linsky • Max Maller • Max O'Connell • Max Rosenak • Maxwell
Fletcher • May Limon Petunia • May Woo • Maya Gurantz • Maya Manian • Maya
Stein • Mayra Quintano • McKay Brown • McKenna Toston • Meagan Linn • Meagan
Patrick • Meaghan Kimball • Meara Day • Meg Beau Harkinson • Meg Beaudet •
Meg Belichick • Meg Donohoe • Meg Donohue • Meg Huth • Meg O'Shaughnessy
• Meg Stern • Meagan Dooley • Megan Hansen • Megan Hines • Megan Kallsltrom
• Megan Keir • Megan Lowery • Megan Malone • Megan Martin • Megan Smith •
Megan Streich • Megan Taylor • Megan Thompson Oliver • Megan Tompkins •
Megan Wagstaffe • Megan Williams • Meghan Adler • Meghan Higgins • Meghan
Nowell • Meghann Williams • Mei-Ling Humphrey • Meika Rouda • Melani
Bombersback • Melanie Abrahams • Melanie Levy • Melanie Roberts • Melanie
Swiercinski • Melinda Gilbert • Melissa Baron • Melissa Chandler • Melissa Federico
• Melissa Graeber • Melissa Ip • Melissa Jones • Melissa Lozano • Melissa Myers •
Melissa Ortiz • Melissa Pocek • Melissa Powar • Melissa Price • Melissa Roberts •
Melissa Severni • Melissa Tan • Melissa Wang • Mena Adlam • Menden Schroeder •
Mendy Holliday • Mercedes Izquierdo Logan • Mercedez Gonzalez • Meredith
Anderson-McDonald • Meredith Barad • Meredith Degyansky • Meredith Heil •
Meredith Kasabian • Meredith Young • Merle Rabine • Merrik Bush • Merrill
Heinrich • Merritt Lander • Metha Klock • Mia Murrietta • Mia Narell • Mia Song •
Miah Jeffra • Micaela Heekin • Micah Pilkington • Michael Abouzelof • Michael
Bailey • Michael Berger • Michael Bina • Michael Blossom • Michael Carson •
Michael Case • Michael Catano • Michael Cavanaugh • Michael Ching • Michael
Chorost • Michael Davidson • Michael DePaul • Michael Disend • Michael Eng •
Michael Ginther • Michael Giotis • Michael Gordon • Michael Haley • Michael
Harkin • Michael Hays • Michael Howerton • Michael Klein • Michael Kramer •
Michael Landis • Michael Luong • Michael Martinez • Michael McCarrin • Michael
McCormick • Michael Nichols • Michael Norton • Michael Ochoa • Michael Pakes •
Michael Pistorio • Michael Principe • Michael Runkle • Michael Shehane • Michal
Ettinger • Michael Tomczyszyn • Michael Tracy • Michael Winters • Michael Zelenko
• Michaela Hulstyn • Michele Armanino • Michele Ayala • Michele Campese •
Michele Fialer • Michele Knapp • Michele Lobatz • Michele Mughannam • Michelle
Allison • Michelle Bennett • Michelle Birch • Michelle Eng • Michelle Flenniken •
Michelle Fritz-Cope • Michelle Grier • Michelle Harris • Michelle Hickey • Michelle
Karell • Michelle Kiefel • Michelle Koehn • Michelle Ma • Michelle Mandolia •
Michelle Mills • Michelle Novak • Michelle Powell • Michelle Powers • Michelle
Quint• Michelle Ruggeri • Michelle Ryan • Michelle Simotas • Michelle Teslik •
Michelle Vizinau-Kvernes • Michelle Yacht • Mielle Sullivan • Miguel Abad • Migiel
de Valencia • Mikaela Dunitz • Mike Adamick • Mike Astaneche • Mike Caputo •
Mike Cho • Mike Di Gino • Mike Levy • Mike Mason • Mike Messner • Mike
Newman • Mike Rabdau • Mike Scagliotti • Mike Schachter • Mike Stein • Mike
Walters • Miles Durrance • Milisa Burke • Milli Frisbie • Mimi Pei Yee Lok • Mindy
Tchieu • Ming Pang • Minna Dubin • Minnie Reichek • Mira-Lisa Katz • Mira Levy
• Miranda Adkins • Miranda Harter • Miranda Kane • Miranda Yaver • Miriam
Greenberger • Miriam Hidalgo • Miriam Posner • Miriam Sorell • Miruna Stanica •
Mischa Rosenberg • Misty Hecht • Misty Dawn-Gaubatz • Misty Osborn • Mitra

Parineh • Miya Reekers • Miyako Abe • Miyoko Ohtake • Moira Williams • Moishe
Brown • Molly Barrett • Molly Kiran • Molly Meng • Molly Mueller • Molly
Niendorf • Molly Parent • Molly Sarle • Molly Stack • Molly Stewart • Molly Thomas
• Molly Walsh • Momo Chang • Monica Contois • Monica Corona • Monica De
Armond • Monica Karaba • Monica Maduro • Monica Pease • Monica Ross • Monika
Jeffress • Monya Baker • Morgan Davis • Morgan Gilliland • Morgan Hopper •
Morgan Jones • Morgan McGuire • Morgan Peirce • Moses Rodriguez • Mulu Amha
• Mysti Berry • Nada Djordjerich • Nada O'Neal • Nada Rastad • Nadia Prupis • Nadir
Jeevanjee • Nadja Blagojevic • Nadya Lev • Nalani Jay • Nancy Chirinos • Nancy
Elgin • Nancy Kivette • Nancy Lopez • Nancy McGee • Nancy Park • Nancy Randall
• Nancy Stait • Nancy Ware • Nancy Zastudil • Nanyoung Jiang • Nanyoung "Jinny"
Ji • Naomi Goldner • Naomi Kosman-Wiener • Naomi Raddatz • Naomi Worthington
• Naomi Zell • Nassim Assefi • Natalia Vigil • Natalie Aleman • Natalie Childress
Smith • Natalie Erickson • Natalie Inouye • Natalie Goldberg • Natalie Guishar •
Natalie Jones • Natalie Linden • Natalie McBride • Natalie McCall • Natalie Moore
• Natalie Powers • Natalie Tsang • Natalie Wolfman • Natasha Lee • Natasha Bronn
• Natasha Opfell • Natasha Warder • Nathalie Peterson • Nathan Adachi • Nathan
Hclurison • Nathan Ie • Nathan Tyler • Nathania Jacobs • Nathaniel Eaton • Nathaniel
Israel • Nathaniel Jue • Natisha Demko • Natty Pilcher • Nawaaz Ahmed • Neal Patel
• Ned Brauer • Nedjo Spaich • Neekta Khorsand • Neeltje Konings • Neha Majithia
• Neil Chazin • Neil Stevenson • Nellie Bowles • Nelly Chauvel • Nelson Graff •
Nelson Jang • Netty Lehn • Neva Beach • Ng Elaine • Ngan Troung • Nicholas Berger
• Nicholas Broten • Nicholas Gattig • Nicholas Maroun • Nicholas Ng • Nicholas Rey
• Nicholas Wallen • Nick Andersen • Nick Cimiluca • Nick Donofrio • Nick Frontino
• Nick Grandy • Nick Howells • Nick Kwaan • Nick Neuman • Nick Noack • Nick
Olsson • Nick Sainati • Nick Simmons • Nick Spencer • Nick Tamburro • Nick Urban
• Nicki Allen • Nicki Pfaff • Nicki Richensin • Nickolas Spencer • Nicky Batill • Nico
Isaac • Nicole Beckley • Nicole Bender • Nicole Bennett • Nicole Boyar • Nicole
Brush • Nicole Burgund • Nicole Calisich • Nicole Dreyfus • Nicole Ertman • Nicole
Gervasio • Nicole Gluckstern • Nicole A. Guintu • Nicole Henares • Nicole Lutton •
Nicole Miller • Nicole O'Hay • Nicole Rainey • Nicole Scher • Nicole Wolfgram •
Nikki Andrews • Nikki Zielinski • Nikolas Sparks • Nima Jahromi • Nina Kohil-
Laven • Nina Krieger • Nina Lacour • Nina Nowack • Nina Torres • Nina Vyas •
Nirmala Nataraj • Nirupam Sinha • Nish Nadaraja • Nisi Baier • Noa Olson • Noah
Hawley • Noah Levine • Noah Martin • Noah Sanders • Noel Gundestrup • Noelle
Duncan • Noelle Rozakos • Nona Caspers • Nona Ikeda • Nonnie Thompson • Nora
Bee • Nora Furst • Nora Hennessy • Nora Mallonee • Nora Rodriguez • Nora Salim
• Nora Toomey • Nora Trice • Noreen Byrne • Nori Hara • Norman Patrick Doyle •
Octavia Driscoll • Ohudy Luna • Olivia Barbee • Olivia Dawes • Olivia Watkins •
Omondi Cleopa • Oona Lyons • Osama Aduib • Oscar Villalon • Oth Khotsimeuang
• Owen Brown • Owen Otto • P. Segal • Padma Gunda • Paige Bierma • Paisley
Strellis • Pam Mayer • Pamela Burdak • Pamela Caul • Pamela Dickson • Pamela
Fortino • Pamela Grisman • Pamela Herbert • Pamela Holm • Pamela Kaye • Paola
Bobadilla • Parissa Ebrahimzadeh • Parvaneh Abbaspour • Pasha Shireen • Pat Allbee
• Pat Murphy • Patricia Callaway • Patricia Kievlan • Patricia Maloney • Patricia
Wong • Patrick Burns • Patrick Coffey • Patrick Fife • Patrick Glynn • Patrick Martin-
Tuite • Patrick Ohslund • Patrick Scott • Patrick Vittek • Patrik Hendrickson • Patsy

Eagan • Patti Cronin • Patti Trimble • Patty Li • Paul Anderson • Paul Barger • Paul Caparotta • Paul Cartier • Paul Chilvers • Paul Glanting • Paul Hagey • Paul Madonna • Paul Oh • Paul Pryor Lorentz • Paul Roccanova • Paul Rueckhaus • Paul Ryan • Paul Sauer • Paul Sigmund • Paul Stelhe • Paul Thomas • Paul Van Slembrouck • Paul Williams • Paul Wrider • Paula Lynch • Paula Murphy • Paula Ponsetto • Paula Rogers • Pavla Popovich • Peanut Wells • Peggy Cartwright • Peggy Ruse • Peggy Simmons • Penelope Robbins • Penelope Thomas • Peretz Partensky • Perry Still • Pete Zuppardo • Peter Finch • Peter Fleming • Peter Kupfer • Peter Lennox-King • Peter Marcus • Peter Maxwell • Peter Prato • Peter Rinzler • Peter Yedidia • Petrice Gaskin • Phil Schaaf • Philip Huang • Philip Kline • Philip Wiatrek • Philipe Irola • Philipp Bourdon • Phillip Nelson • Phoebe Hyde • Phoebe Morgan • Phoebe Westwood • Phyllis Mason • Pia Shah • Pippa Wright • Pinar Buyukkurt • PJ Brown • PK McBee • Polly Conway • Poz Lang • Prasanthi Persad • Priya Kailath • Priscilla Washington • Quinn Norton • Quintessa Matranga • Quressa Robinson • Rachael Cunningham • Rachael Goop • Rachael Lipsetts • Rachael Solomon • Rachana Vajjhala • Rachel Bernard • Rachel Baudoin • Rachel Been • Rachel Biello • Rachel Blumberg • Rachel Bovee • Rachel Boyes • Rachel Brylawski • Rachel Chalmers • Rachel Duncan • Rachel Elliott • Rachel Goldstein • Rachel Greenberger • Rachel Hodara • Rachel Howard • Rachel Hudson • Rachel Kast • Rachel Kauder Nalebuff • Rachel Kast • Rachel Kotkin • Rachel Krapf • Rachel Lefkowitz • Rachel Leibrock • Rachel Lyon • Rachel Marcus • Rachel Max • Rachel McNassor • Rachel Richardson • Rachel Rubin • Rachel Sadler • Rachel Shearer • Rachel Simpson • Rachel Schwartz • Rachel Spiegel • Rachel Steinberg • Rachel Weidinger • Rachel Williams • Rachel Wong • Rachel Zurer • Rae Draizen • Raegan Test • Raema Quam • Rafael Silberblatt • Rafael Vranizan • Rafaela Minkowsky • Rahmin Sarabi • Rainier Sanchez • Raja Shah • Rajee Karunaratne • Ralph Leon Gootee • Ran Bolton • Randi Abel • Randall Johnson • Randy Wilson • Ranee Zaporski • Raphael Crawford-Marks • Raphael di Donato • Raquel Aceves • Rashid Dhana • Ravi K • Ray Lent • Ray Mertens • Ray Rubin • Rayna Goldman • Rebbeca Hersh • Rebbeca Kaden • Rebbeca Poretsky • Rebbeca Rubin • Rebecca Beal • Rebecca Best • Rebecca Black • Rebecca Blake • Rebecca Blatt • Rebecca Farivar • Rebecca Fenton • Rebecca Foster • Rebecca Golman • Rebecca Kraut • Rebecca Marshall • Rebecca Oksner • Rebecca Pederson • Rebecca Poretsky • Rebecca Rice • Rebecca Schonberg • Rebecca Seifert • Rebecca Shapiro • Rebecca Siegel • Rebecca Sills • Rebecca Stern • Rebecca Szeto • Rebecca Wetherbee • Rebecca Winterer • Rebekah sFergusson • Rebekah Kane • Rebekah Werth • Reese McLaughlin • Regina Ernst • Reid Hansen • Reid Ulrich • Relicque Lott • Renae Skarin • Renato Teroy • Rene Kamm • Renee Ashbaugh • Renee Berger • Renee Infelise • Reneé Summerfield • Renina Jarmon • Renny Talianchich • Rex Flores • Reya Sehgal • Reyhan Harmanci • Reynard Seifert • Ria Fay-Berquist • Ricardo Zahra • Richard Enriquez • Richard Griswold • Richard Kimura • Richard Trudeau • Richard Zuckerman • Richelle McClain • Rick Johnson • Rick Opaterny • Rick Trushel • Rick Zuzow • Rickey Kelly • Ricky Musci • Rikki Ward • Rick Wolfgram • Riley McLaughlin • Rin Nakamura • Rinee Shah • Rio Roth-Barreiro • Risa Monsen • Risa Nye Ritika Aulakh, Riva Gardner, Rob Ehle, Rob Smith, Rob Tocalino, Robbie Beers, Robbie Marlin, Robbie Torney, Robert Burnside, Robert Gill, Robert Glushko, Robert Luhn, Robert McDiarmid, Robert Merryman, Robert Palmer, Robert Pollack, Robert Rosenthal, Robert Selna, Robert Solley, Robert

Watson, Roberta D'Alois, Roberta Lawrinksy, Robin Galguera, Robin O'Malley, Robin Pam, Robin Sloan, Rita Tucker Robin Wilkey, Robyn Kick, Robyn Moller, Robyn White, Rodd Aubrey, Rodney Koeneke, Roisin Reardon, Roland Goity, Romy Ruukel, Ron Piovesan, Ron Wilko, Rona Jin, Ronna Tanenbaum, Ronnie Misra, Rorie Oliver, Rosa Alvarado, Rosa Boshier, Rose Kleiner, Rose Tully, Roselyn Roark, Rosemary Slattery, Rosey Rouhana, Rosha Motti, Rosie Ke Garsmeur, Rosie Lewis, Ross Borden, Ross Burgstead, Ross Trudeau, Roxane Izadian, Roxanne Anzelc, Roxanne Brodeur, roxanne izadian, Rozelle Polido, Ruby Bremer, Ruby Kalson-Bremer, Ruby Veridiano-Ching, Rucker Alex, Ruggero Pergher, Rushelle Carriere, Russell Bentley, Russell Dillon, Russell Latham, Russell Ward, Rusti Icenogel, Ruth Johnson, Ruth Kalnitsky, Ruth Osorio, Ruth Rainero, Ruth Rosenthal, Ruth Young, Ryan Browne, Ryan Foley, Ryan Folley, Ryan Fuller, Ryan Germick, Ryan Kennedy, Ryan Kiick, Ryan Knapp, Ryan MacDonald, Ryan Mammarella, Ryan McFadden, Ryan McIntyre, Ryan Moore, Ryan Moskal, Ryan Novack, Ryan O'Donnell, Ryan Pittington, Ryan Purdy, Ryan Teitman, Ryo Chijiwa, Saadia Malik, Sabina Rocke, Sabrina Lemke, Sabrina Mutukisna, Sabrina Ramos, Sabrina Tom, Sadie Beaudet, Sage Romano, Sahar Shirazi, Sajad Shaterian, Salil Shah, Salina Yong, Salinda Tyson, Sally Baggett, Sally Haims, Sally Hughes, Sally (Wen Wen) Mao, Sally Scopa, Sally Stillman, Salome Milstead, Sam Britton, Sam Feignbaum, Sam Felsing, Sam Gray, Sam Powers, Sam Riviere, Sam Silverstein, Sam Taxy, Samantha Barclay-Saxon, Samantha Dakin, Samantha Edwards-Cordova, Samantha Hall, Samantha Jones, Samantha Marx, Samantha McCarthy, Samantha Morgan, Samantha Morrow, Samantha Remeika, Samantha Rubenstein, Samantha Schoech, Samantha Tackeff, Samantha Tieu, Samay Gheewala, Samson Zadmehran, Samuel Christian, Samuel Meehan, Sandee Bisson, Sandi Gaytan, Sandra Cardoza, Sandra Cupford, Sandra Handler, Sandra Kelley, Sandra Meyer, Sandra Ogle, Sandra Square, Sandra Staklis, Sandra Stringer, Sara Faith Alterman, Sandy Biagi, Sandy Pierson, Sara Alsop, Sara Ansari, Sara Bilandzija, Sara Bilandzja, Sara Bright, Sara Chimene-Weiss, Sara Deneweth, Sara Gaiser, Sara Mann, Sara Marshall, Sara Moncivais, Sara Moore, Sara Press, Sara Randazzo, Sara Safriet, Sara Suddes, Sarah Ackerley, Sarah Adler, Sarah Anderson, Sarah Boswell, Sarah Bruhns, Sarah Buishas, Sarah Burgundy, Sarah Rose Butler, Sarah Cassedy, Sarah Chihaya, Sarah Christenson, Sarah Cooke, Sarah Dyen, Sarah Dennis, Sarah Dulaney, Sarah Fielding, Sarah Fontaine, Sarah Gagnon, Sarah B. Gibson, Sarah Gilman-Short, Sarah Glover, Sarah Godfrey, Sarah Grierson, Sarah Gross, Sarah Gurman, Sarah Henderson, Sarah Henson, Sarah Hobin, Sarah Lochlann Jain, Sarah Key, Sarah Keefe, Sarah Knup, Sarah Kobrinsky-Kleinzahler, Sarah Lahey, Sarah Lee, Sarah Leslie, Sarah Lewin, Sarah Lidgus, Sarah Lounsbury, Sarah Lynch, Sarah Malashock, Sarah Marloff, Sarah McCabe, Sarah McCoy, Sarah Melikian, Sarah Million, Sarah Pape, Sarah Peterson, Sarah Phan, Sarah Ramey, Sarah Rhyins, Sarah Rich, Sarah Richardson, Sarah Roberts, Sarah Roos, Sarah Savage, Sarah Schlosseer, Sarah Schlosser, Sarah Shectman, Sarah Nevada Smith, Sarah Stone, Sarah Tannehill, Sarah West Ulmer, Sarah Vallette, Sarah Wells, Sarah Williams, Sarah Woo, Sarah Wulfeck. Sarahjane Sacchetti, Sari Gelzer, Sasha Buscho, Sasha Kinney, Sasha Strackhouse, Sasha Swartzman, Sativa January, Saurabhi Singh, Savannah Thompson, Scott Benbow, Scott Buros, Scott Goodenow, Scott Gowin, Scott Grinsell, Scott James, Scott Knippelmeir, Scott Lambridis, Scott Loganbill, Scott Manus, Scott Marengo, Scott McLin, Scott Moore, Scott Onak, Scott

Recchia, Scott Service, Scott Smith, Scott Walker, Scott Wardell, Scott Zorsch, Sean Beaudoin, Sean Richard Conroy, Sean Hanratty, Sean Houlihan, Sean Paul Keating, Sean Mackay, Sean Messenger, Sean Rougean, Sean Williford, Sean Young, Sebastian Vermette, Sekai Chideya, Selena Simmons-Duffin, Sepi Alavi, Setareh Banisadr, Seth Endo, Seth Fischer, Seth Linden, Seth Liss, Seth Mausner, Seth Rosenthal, Seth Williams, Shaan Kirpalani, Shaheen Bilgrami, Shai Ben-David, Shamala Gallagher, Shana Mahaffey, Shane Hildebrandt, Shane Michalik, Shane Orzechowski, Shane Papatolicas, Shannon Allen, Shannon Bryant, Shannon Cogen, Shannon DeJong, Shannon Dodge, Shannon Grant, Shannon Grassmen, Shannon Rice, Shannon Ryan, Shannon Short, Shannon Webber, Shannon Wheeler, Shannon Wianecki, Shari Kizirian, Shari Leskowitz, Shari Rubin, Sharmin Nordien Jackson, Sharon Avesar, Sharon Cohen, Sharon Foldes, Sharon Ly, Sharon Mckellar, Sharon Rosenfeld, Sharon Traavers, Shaun Archer, Shawn O'Connor, Shawna Thompson, Shayna Lewis, Sheau-Wha Mou-Keefe, Sheehan Lunt, Sheela Kumar, Sheena Simpson, Sheila Nazzaro, Shelby Polakoff, Shelly Leachman, Shelly Ronen, Shelly Willard, Sheri Mitchell, Sherri Morr, Sherisse Steward, Sherry Rahmani, Sheryl Ellis, Shilpa Duvoor, Shira Levine, Shirazi Sahar, Shirin Houshangi, Shireen Pasha, Shloka Mangaram, Shyla Batliwalla, Sidath Perera, Sidra Durst, Sidrah Gibbs, Sierra Melcher, Sigrid Anderson, Sigrid Sutter, Silan Yip, Simon Hodgson, Simon Smithson, Simon West, Simone Gelfand, Simone Morris-Martin, Sinclair Wu, Sindya Bahnoo, Sita Bhaumik, Sky Chari, Sky Madden, Slaven Svetinovic, Sobrina Tung, Soha Al-Jurf, Soleil David, Solidad Decosta, Solveig Pederson, Sona Avakian, Sonali Kulkarni, Sondra Hall, Sondra Schreibman, Sonia Belasco, Sonia Faleiro, Sonia Minden, Sonya Palay, Sonya Real, Soo-Jin Sohn, Sophia Kim, Sophia Renn, Sophia Sherwood, Sophia Yap, Sophie Dresser, Sophie Klimt, Sophie Sills, Soraya Haas, Soraya Okuda, Soru Gray, Spencer Cronk, Spencer Morris, Squid B. Varilekova, Stacey Hendren, Stacey Palevsky, Stacia Priscilla, Stacy Barrett, Stacy Cohen, Stacy Muccino, Stacy Redd, Stan Heller, Star Van, Stardust Darkmatterji, Starla Estrada, Stefia Maxwell, Stefanie Chinn, Stefanie Olsen, Stephanie Campbell, Stephanie DiLibero, Stephanie Doeing, Stephanie Foo, Stephanie Gilmann, Stephanie Hammon, Stephanie Kinser, Stephanie Kinnear, Stephanie Klein, Stephanie Kurteff, Stephanie Lawrence, Stephanie Mantica, Stephanie Moore, Stephanie Morgan, Stephanie Pau, Stephanie Philson, Stephanie Pinkham, Stephanie Pullen, Stephanie Rich, Stephanie Rue, Stephanie Schenkel, Stephanie Secrest, Stephanie Watanabe, Stephanie Witherspoon, Stephany Ventura, Stephen Barlow, Stephen Backer, Stephen Elliott, Stephen Emerson, Stephen Grafensne, Stephen Labovsky, Stephen Meads, Stephen Meuris, Stephen Miller, Stephen On, Stephen Rosenshein, Stephen Wade, Stephie Gregory, Stern Rebecca, Steve Blumenthal, Steve Dildarian, Steve Kustra, Steve Medina, Steve Reidy, Steve Ruston, Steve Souryal, Steven Gdula, Steven Shimmon, Stewart McBride, Sudeshna Dev, Sue Pierce, Sue Pirri, Sue Yang, Suejean Kim, Suji Kong, Sukey Bernard, Sumaya Agha, Sumeet Bakshi, Summer Block, Summer Pendle, Sunil Patel, Sunny Yan, Susan Bach, Susan Banie, Susan Gram, Susan Gray, Susan Hahn, Susan Hara, Susan Jung, Susan Karem, Susan Coelius Keplinger, Susan Kramer, Susan Meister, Susan O'Connor, Susan Stranger, Susan "Suzie" Stevens, Susan Tu, Susan Yao-Tresguerres, Susanna Fryer, Susanna Kittredge, Susanna Schell, Susannah Carson, Susanne Stolzenberg, Susie Britton, Susie Cagel, Susie Nadler, Susie Zavala, Suzanne Barber, Suzanne Connolly, Suzanne Dennis-Martineau,

Suzanne Ginsburg, Suzanne Kleid, Suzanne Leupold, Suzanne O'Kelly/Richards, Suzanne Scholten, Suzette Duncan, Suzie Hill, Sven, Sydney Sattell, Sydney Schaub, Sylvia Sommer, Tabitha Steager, Tae Kim, Talia Muscarella, Talla Wesely, Tamar Sberlo, Tamara Bock, Tamara Little, Tamara Micner, Tamela Ekstrom, Tammy Dorje, Tammy Fortin, Tamsen Merrill, Tania Kentenjian, Tania Padilla, Tanu Wakefield, Tanya Clark, Tanya Gallardo, Tanya Madoff, Tanya Marshall, Tanya Wilkinson, Tara Bradley, Tara Brown, Tara Daly, Tara Ebrahimi, Tara Misra, Tara Mocsny, Tara Ramadan, Tarek Haffar, Taryn McCabe, Tasha Carvell, Tasha Marie Glen, Tasneem Kapadia, Tatevik Garibyan, Tavia Stewart, Tayler Buffington, Taylor Chenette, Taylor Garland, Taylor Harrison, Taylor Jacobson, Taylor Landry, Taylor Pasi, Taylour Nelson, Taysa Charnell, Ted Everson, Ted Snyderman, Terence McKeown, Terence Potter, Teresa Brennan, Teresa Cotsirilos, Teresa Gurtiza, Teri Hu, Terri Bogaards, Terri Farley, Terry Diggs, Terry Oestreicher, Terry Pan, Terry Ross, Terry E. Wilder, Tess McCarthy, Tess Patalano, Tessa Melvin, Tessa Stuart, Tessa White, Thalia Gigrenzer, Thao Nguyen, Theresa Ganz, Theresa Lee, Theresa Preston-Werner, Therese Mitros, Therese Quinlan, Thia Bonidies, Thomas Michael Bailey, Thomas Brannon, Thomas Brierly, Thomas Chupein, Thomas Gorman, Thomas King, Thomas Thornhill, Thomson Nguyen, Tia Woodward, Tibora Girczyc-Blum, Tienlon Ho, Tierney Henderson, Tiffany Lin, Tiffani Carter, Tiffany Chen, Tiffany Chow, Tiffany Clarke, Tiffany Dempton, Tiffany Hsu, Tiffany Kats, Tiffany Maleshefski, Tiffany Shlain, Tika Hall, Tim Adams, Tim Anderson, Tim Archuleta, Tim Billings, Tim Chu, Tim Chupein, Tim Coleman, Tim Floreen, Tim James, Tim Lewis, Tim McAtee, Tim McNerney, Tim Parsa, Tim Ratanapreukskul, Tim Tolka, Tim Wagstaffe, Timothy Barry, Timothy David Marsolais, Timothy McCormack, Timothy Wagstaffe, Tina Cheng, Tina Lee, Tine Zhong, Toba Strauss, Tobin O'Donnel, Tobyn Smith, Todd Carnam, Todd Chapman, Todd Perumal, Todd Pound, Todd von Ammon, Tom Annese, Tom Chiappari, Tom Durst, Tom Edwards, Tom Gorman, Tom Hoynes, Tom Kealey, Tom Kelly, Tom Lagatta, Tom Magrino, Tom Molanphy, Tom Wilkinson, Tommy Flynn, Tomoko Ferguson, Tony Nunes, Tony Gabriel Prendez, Tonyanna Borkovi, Townsend Walker,Tracey Clark, Tracey Samuelson, Tracy Barreiro, Tracy Blanchard, Tracy Clark-Flory, Tracy Deluca, Tracy Gallagher, Tracy Lynn Schafer, Tracy Seeley, Tracy Valenzi, Tracy White, Travis Wainman, Travis Wallis, Trent Fereria, Trevor Kuski, Trevor Stern, Tricia Sweeney, Trish Murphy, Tristan Volpe, Tristanne Walliser, Troy Wiliams, Trudy Fisher, Tuesday Moon, Ty Jones, Tyler Ortman, Tze Yeoh, Udeitha Srimushnam, Uri Lopatin, Vail Shulman, Valduna Keren, Valerie Ibarra, Valerie Witte, Van Nguyen, Vance Ingalls, Vanessa Grahl, Vanessa Heckman, Vanessa Hsu, Vanessa Hua, Vanessa Lindlaw, Vanessa Maida, Vanessa Marsh, Vanessa Norton, Vanessa Pena, Vanessa Raney, Vanessa Reid, Vanessa Rose, Vanessa Saunders, Vanessa Tom, Vanessa Touset, Vanessa Waring, Vanessa Weber, Vanitha Sankaran, Vaughn Shields, Vauhini Vara, Vendela Vida, Veronica Dakota, Veronica Kavass, Veronica Padilla, Veronica Peterson, Vi T. Le, Vicki Vaughn, Vickie Chang, Victor Oliveros, Victor Vazquez, Victoria Buonanno, Victoria Cardozo, Victoria Emery, Victoria Hinshaw, Victoria Legg, Victoria Sanchez, Victoria Thomas, Victoria Valenzuela, Victoria Wieldt, Vidya Sryanarayanan, Vincent Wong, Viola Or, Virginia Benitez, Virginia Cardozo, Virginia Miller, Virginia O'Brien, Virginia Rider, Virginia Woolworth, Viv Grande, Vivecca Yong Tim, Vivek Tata, Vivian Triantafillou, Wade Peerman, Walt Opie, Wan-Yin Tang, Wanda Mazur,

Wandee Pryor, Wendy Freedman, Wendy Hill, Wendy Trevino, Wendy Wu, Wesley Hall, Whitney Morgan, Whitney Phaneuf, Whitney Riter, Wilbert Williams, Will Berry, Will Craven, Will Fehlhaber, Will Rutland, Will Sargent, Willem Van Lancker, William Bloxham, William Cornwell, William Dean, William Gallagher, William Mee, William Pentney, William Warne, Willis Tsai, Willow Mata, Wilson Hu, Windy Ferges, Wistar MacLaren, Wyatt Hunter, Wynene Wilson, Xander Piper, Xavier Gomez, Yael Meromy, Yakira Teitel, Yale Kim, Yasmin Nestlen, Yenny Martin, Yosh Han, Yoshi Salaverry, Yousef Al-Balouchi, Yusuf Ali, Yvette Bozzini, Zach Bloom, Zach Cohen, Zach Koch, Zack Kushner, Zack Onisko, Zack Stern-Walker, Zach Steinman, Zach Wyner, Zachary Amendt, Zachary Aslanian-Williams, Zachary Wyatt Zan (Alexander) Cukor, Zachary Gobst, Zachary Krane, Zachary Shore, Zandra Urbina, Zane Morris, Zara Axelrod, Zeeda Anderson, Zeke Harrington, Zena Caputo, Zev Rubin, Zoe Brock, Zoe Catsiff, Zoe Finkel, Zoe Ganim, Zoe Leverant, Zoe Luhtala, Zoe Pinfold, Zoe Strominger, Zoe Torres, Zoe Urann, Zoey Burrows, Zulema Summerfield, Zmira Zilkha

HOW TO GET INVOLVED

That list looks huge, but the need from the students we serve is even bigger. We are always looking for more volunteers to help us with our programming. Also, we can always use more volunteers with software skills, advanced writing skills, or advanced design skills. It's easy to become a volunteer and a bunch of fun to actually do it. Please fill out our online form to let us know you'd like to be a part of what we do: *826valencia.org/get-involved/volunteer.*

826 NATIONAL

826 Valencia's success has spread across the country. Under the umbrella of 826 National, writing and tutoring centers have opened up in seven more cities. If you would like to learn more about other 826 programs, please visit the following websites.

826 National	**826 DC**	**826 NYC**
826national.org	*826dc.org*	*826nyc.org*
826 Boston	**826 LA**	**826 Seattle**
826boston.org	*826la.org*	*826seattle.org*
826 CHI	**826 Michigan**	**826 Valencia**
826chi.org	*826michigan.org*	*826valencia.org*

The Programs of
826 Valencia

We are so proud of the student writing collected in this edition of the *826 Quarterly*. It is the result of countless hours of hard work by students and teachers alike. We are also endlessly inspired by our hardworking tutors, all of whom make the following programs possible. If you have not yet visited 826 Valencia, or if it has been a while, please do come by to see us—we'll treat you to a good mopping, free of charge.

AFTER-SCHOOL TUTORING

Five days a week, 826 Valencia is packed with students who come in for free one-on-one tutoring. Some students need help with homework. Others come in to work on ambitious extracurricular projects, such as novels and plays. We're particularly proud of our thriving services and support for young students learning English.

FIELD TRIPS

Three or four times a week, 826 Valencia welcomes an entire class of students for a morning of high-energy learning. Classes may request a custom-designed curriculum on a subject they've been studying, such as playwriting, or choose from one of our five field-trip plans. Our most popular is the Storytelling & Bookmaking field trip. In two hours, the students write, illustrate, and publish their own books. They leave with keepsake stories and a newfound excitement for writing.

IN-SCHOOL PROGRAMMING

826 Valencia's In-School Programming reaches the greatest number of students, as we go into public schools across the city to support teachers with their curricula and give students individualized attention. While collaborating with teachers on their programs, tutors help students with the expository and creative writing inherent in each project.

WORKSHOPS

826 Valencia offers workshops almost every day of the year at the 826 Writing Lab. Workshops are devoted to teaching a variety of skills, including, but not limited to, comic-book writing, podcasting, and SAT essay writing for high-school seniors. They are taught by professionals in the literary arts in classes of twelve to fifteen students, so each student gets the individual attention he or she needs. At the end of the workshop, the students' work is read live to an audience at 826, or recorded and put online, made into a short film, or most often, made into a fine chapbook that they each get to keep and we sell in our store.

SUMMER PROGRAMS

During the summer, our tutoring program caters to elementary school students who are reading and writing below grade level. Our project-based curriculum focuses on boosting literacy skills and confidence over six weeks of activities. We also host an intensive writing camp for high school students, in which campers write all day, every day, and work with celebrated authors and artists such as Michael Chabon, ZZ Packer, and Spike Jonze.

WRITERS' ROOMS

Our Writers' Rooms at Everett Middle School and James Lick Middle School are warm, in-school satellites where our volunteers serve every student in the school over the course of the year. These spaces allow teachers to reduce their class sizes and students to receive the one-on-one attention that leads to success.

Student Publications

826 Valencia produces a variety of publications, each of which contains work written by students in our various programs. Some are professionally printed and nationally distributed, others are glued together here and sold in the pirate store. These projects represent some of the most exciting work at 826 Valencia, as they enable Bay Area students to experience a world of publishing not otherwise available to them. Students of 826 wrote for the following publications:

Beyond Stolen Flames, Forbidden Fruit, and Telephone Booths (2011) is a collection of essays and short stories written by fifty-three juniors and seniors at June Jordan School for Equity in which young writers explore the role of myth in our world today. Students wrote pieces of fiction and nonfiction, retelling old myths, creating new ones, celebrating everyday heroes, and recognizing the stories that their families have told over and over. With a foreword by Khaled Hosseini, the result is a collection with a powerful message about the stories that have shaped students' perspectives and the world they know.

We the Dreamers (2010) is a collection of essays by fifty-one juniors at John O'Connell High School reflecting on what the American Dream means to them. The students recount stories about family, home, immigration, hardship, and the hopes of their generation, as well as those of the generation that raised them. The result is a firsthand account of these essayists' often-complicated relationship with our national ethos that is insightful, impassioned, surprising, and of utmost importance to our understanding of what the American Dream means for their generation.

Show of Hands (2009) is a collection of stories and essays written by fifty-four juniors and seniors at Mission High School. It amplifies the students' voices as they reflect on one of humanity's most revered guides for moral behavior: the Golden Rule. Whether speaking about global issues, street violence, or the way to behave among friends and family, the voices of these young essayists are brilliant, thoughtful, and, most of all, urgent.

Thanks and Have Fun Running the Country (2009) is a collection of letters penned by our after-school tutoring students to newly elected President Obama. In this collection, which arrived at inauguration time, there's loads of advice for the president, often hilarious, sometimes heartfelt, and occasionally downright practical. The letters have been featured in the *New York Times,* the *San Francisco Chronicle,* and on *This American Life.*

Seeing Through the Fog (2008) is a guidebook written by seniors from Gateway High School, and it explores San Francisco from tourist, local, and personal perspectives. Both whimsical and factually accurate, the pieces in this collection take the reader to the places that teenagers know best, from taquerias to skate spots to fashionable shops that won't break your budget.

Exactly (2007) is a hardbound book of colorful stories for children ages nine to eleven. This collection of fifty-six narratives by students at Raoul Wallenberg Traditional High School is illustrated by forty-three professional artists. It passes on lessons that teenagers want the next generation to know.

 Inspired by magical realism, students at Galileo Academy of Science and Technology produced *Home Wasn't Built in a Day* (2006), a collection of short stories based on family myths and legends. With a foreword by actor and comedian Robin Williams, the book comes alive through powerful student voices that explore just what it is that makes a house a home.

 *I Might Get Somewhere: Oral Histories of Immigration and Migration* (2005) exhibits an array of student-recorded oral narratives about moving to San Francisco from other parts of the United States and all over the world. Acclaimed author Amy Tan wrote the foreword to this compelling collection of personal stories by Balboa High School students. All these narratives shed light on the problems and pleasures of finding one's life in new surroundings.

 Written by thirty-nine students at Thurgood Marshall Academic High School, *Waiting to Be Heard: Youth Speak Out About Inheriting a Violent World* (2004) addresses violence and peace on a personal, local, and global scale. With a foreword by Isabel Allende, the book combines essays, fiction, poetry, and experimental writing to create a passionate collection of student expression.

 *Talking Back: What Students Know About Teaching* (2003) is a book that delivers the voices of the class of 2004 from Leadership High School. In reading the book, previously being used as a required-reading textbook at San Francisco State University and Mills College, you will understand the relationships students want with their teachers, how students view classroom life, and how the world affects students.

826 Valencia also publishes scores of chap-books each semester. These collections of writing primarily come from two sources: our volunteer-taught evening and weekend workshops, and our in-school projects where students work closely with tutors to edit their writing. Designed and printed right at 826 Valencia, the resulting chapbooks range from student-penned screenplays to collections of bilingual poetry.

PUBLICATIONS FOR STUDENTS & TEACHERS

Don't Forget to Write (2005) contains fifty-four of the best lesson plans used in workshops taught at 826 Valencia, 826NYC, and 826LA, giving away all of our secrets for making writing fun. Each lesson plan was written by its original workshop teacher, including Jonathan Ames, Aimee Bender, Dave Eggers, Erika Lopez, Julie Orringer, Jon Scieszka, Sarah Vowell, and many others. If you are a parent or a teacher, this book is meant to make your life easier, as it contains enthralling and effective ideas to get your students writing. It can also be used as a resource for the aspiring writer.

The Store at 826 Valencia

"Definitely one of the top five pirate stores I've been to recently." —DAVID BYRNE

What happens in the store at 826 Valencia? Many have said that upon entering San Francisco's only independent pirate-supply store, they get a sensation of déjà vu. Others walk in and feel at once the miracle work of an unseen hand. And there are those whose eyes bulge and shrink simultaneously, their thoughts so convoluted that they are unable to shout or mutter the question that most plagues them: "What is this place?"

PIRATE STORE STAFF & VOLUNTEERS

Staff
Iris Alden
Jessica Tzur
Justin Carder
Samantha Riley
Soraya Okuda
Hannah Kingsley-Ma
Amy Langer

Volunteers
Eleven, Inc.
Reya Hart

Window Display Artists
Iris Alden
Justin Carder
Lauren Hartman
Lauren Mulkey
Liz Worthy
Lynn Rubenzer
Sita Bhaumik
Kristen Libero

The Sad, Sad Life of Lobsterman

Presented in conjunction with
**IRIS ALDEN & JUSTIN CARDER
AND THE SOCIETY FOR SAD MUSEUMS**

with generous funding provided by
**A GENERIC FACIAL TISSUE COMPANY,
THE STATE OF MARYLAND
DEPARTMENT OF FISH AND GAME,
AND ANONYMOUS DONORS**

Every two months or so, we change the items in the window display so as to fool passersby into thinking we're a different store (certainly not the one where they were so rudely mopped last week). For a while we'd just switch up the letters in our name and that was good enough. But over the years, we've had to come up with more and more elaborate ways to fool the people of San Francisco, like a cannon that shoots gold coins, a dinghy floating in a sea with pterodactyls flying around, a giant squid, et cetera. One of the strangest, and surely the saddest thing we ever had was this display, "The Sad, Sad Life of Lobsterman." In it was a life-size replica of a man who also happened to be a lobster, artifacts from his life and captions describing them. Here is a sampling of some of the items and their sad, sad stories.

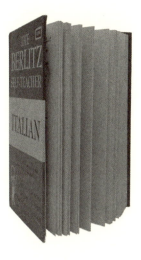

Italian Dictionaries

Various Locations; Mid-Late 20th Century

Over the course of his life, L. learned to speak and read Italian fluently in hopes of one day visiting Italy. There was one man who spoke Italian in town who worked down the street from the watch repair store. L. would often linger longer than he needed to over paper towels or cat food, just to listen in on the man's conversation with himself. There were never any other Italians in the store (wrong neighborhood, maybe?), so the man spent all his time talking to himself, making comments about customers. Mostly rude comments, actually. L. decided that to reveal that he also spoke Italian would really mess with the old man's ability to speak freely about whomever he pleased whenever he pleased. So he vowed to never let on that he understood what the man said. The only person who ever actually heard L. speak in Italian was his wife, who was once woken up by L. mumbling Italian verb conjugations in his sleep. She had no way of knowing this, but his pronunciation was flawless.

Pocket Watch

Gift from Deceased Grandfather; 1945

L.'s grandfather, Aleksandr P_____, was accidentally murdered by a nearsighted assassin on March 15th, 1938 in the back of a taxi intended for the prime minister of Latvia. L. was eight years old. He did not know his grandfather well, other than the old man came from the Bialowieza Forest in Poland or Belarus (no one was sure exactly) to America on the back of a floating donkey cart, and once tried to teach five-year-old L. how to smoke a cigar while he waited for his mother to pick him up after kindergarten at the watch repair shop. Papa's will indicated the watch repair shop would go to L.'s father, and the watch to L.—however, L. never actually received it. The watch was gambled away by L.'s father a week after Papa's death and replaced with this much cheaper replica. L. was never told this, and believed the watch to be authentic all his life.

Horse Diorama

Possible Christmas Gift; c. 1934

L. carried this strange relic of his childhood with him his whole life. No one knows exactly why. He never spoke about it, never mentioned any special interest in it, or in horses or in diorama-making. Once his wife threw it away, thinking it had belonged to one of the boys after they'd moved away to college. L. found it missing and dug through the city dump for a whole work day just to find it. He asked to be buried with it. No one could find it at the time, but his sons have vowed that if he is ever exhumed for any reason—like, if the cemetery needs to be moved to accommodate condominiums or a sports field or something—they will go together and make things right. For now it resides here, just another mystery in the very mysterious, sad life of Lobsterman.

Camera Collection

Various Locations; Mid to Late 20th Century

L. enjoyed taking pictures more than almost anything in his life. He took pictures of sunsets and of his children, of his wife, of the beaches he liked to go to and the foods he enjoyed. He obsessively documented nearly every moment of his family's life—once even taking pictures of the family watching a slide-show of other pictures he'd taken. This need to document often got in the way of L. enjoying some of the more visceral thrills of life. He preferred taking pictures of his children running around or swinging on a swing to actually pushing them or running around with them. To take pictures of waves crashing rather than to feel the crash on his exoskeleton. After his death, many of the photos were split among the children. About a dozen were purchased by the author of these exhibit labels at a flea market. Four for a dollar. The vast majority of the collection has been recycled.

Handsaw

Unknown; Early 20th Century

This is not L.'s saw. He never used a saw like this in his life. Once he'd been taken by his father to cut down a Christmas tree but was too cold to get out of the car. No one knows how it got into the exhibit. Possibly left by the preparators by accident. Or maybe there were just too many pedestals. Or it was just already in the window, left from some previous window display that had some kind of woodsy theme. Anyone's guess is as good as ours.

NOTE: If you are the owner of this saw, please inquire within. Be prepared to present valid identification and any receipt or proof-of-purchase you have for the saw. If you do not have any of those items, be prepared to wrestle for it.

Editorial Board Outro

GINA CARGAS * *Age 19*
Cornell University

A CONFESSION

In this afterword, you will find the following: musings on writing, shameless glorification of 826 Valencia, and perhaps a little self-indulgent boasting.

However, to maintain some element of suspense, I will tell you that this afterword also contains a confession. At one point in my 826 career, I committed a horrible crime. Not exactly a crime in the regular sense, but certainly a crime that our dear editor Mr. Blue would frown upon. You could, of course, skip to the end and discover what this shameful misdeed was, but I'd rather you read on. Anyway, let's get started.

My mother first dragged me to 826 Valencia at the age of eleven. I was beyond reluctant—after all, why would I want to go to class after school? Not yet in my rebellious phase, I was coerced into attending a workshop during which I wrote a story from the perspectives of seven pieces of food, and, well, I never really left. You'd think they'd be sick me of me by now, but for unclear reasons 826 hired me this summer as part of the Alumni Internship Program.

Now, instead of writing terrible angsty poetry or furiously debating the merits of a short story, I spend my days writing space-themed lesson plans, helping with outreach, and, of course, convincing third graders that they really don't need to sharpen their pencil for the fifteenth time today. I've learned a lot, from how to plan a fundraiser to the location of the Swiffer pads to the best way to answer the question "Do you think Lionel Messi or Jesus would be better at soccer?"

Essentially—and I mean this in the cheesiest, most sentimental way possible—826 has played an enormous role in my life, and I am eternally grateful. Without this place (here comes the self-indulgent boasting), I probably never would have ended up writing for three different publications in college or learned how to succesfully teach a seven-year-old how to write a haiku. I wouldn't know nearly as much as I do about writing or editing or pirates. And I probably wouldn't have a summer job.

And now that you have waded through my obsessive ranting about 826, it is time for the confession. Here goes:

Somewhere in my room, there is a copy of *The Importance of Being Earnest* that I borrowed from 826 in 2007. There. I said it. I'm sorry, everyone. I'm sorry to the high schoolers who missed out because of my forgetfulness. I'm sorry to whoever donated the book. I'm sorry to Justin, mainly because he gave me a free poster last week and I so clearly don't deserve it.

So, element of suspense maintained? No? Alas. In any case, thank you so much for reading this collection. Remember the adventures of Mike the lizard, the trials of Adrian the turnip-man, and the rabid ghost pulling pranks on Justin Bieber. I know I will.

What's Hiding Under Your Mattress?

Whether it's loose change or heaps of cash, a donation of any size will help 826 Valencia continue to offer a wide variety of FREE literacy and publishing programs to Bay Area youths. We would greatly appreciate your support.

Please make a donation at:
826valencia.org/get-involved/donate
Or mail a check to:
826 Valencia Street
San Francisco, California 94110

Your donation is tax deductible. What a plus!
Thank you!